Empty
Bed
Blues

WILLIAM WALL

NEW ISLAND

EMPTY BED BLUES
First published in 2023 by
New Island Books
Glenshesk House
10 Richview Office Park
Clonskeagh
Dublin D14 V8C4
Republic of Ireland
www.newisland.ie

Print ISBN: 978-1-84840-883-8
Ebook ISBN: 978-1-84840-884-5

British Library Cataloguing in Publication Data. A CIP catalogue record for this book is available from the British Library.

Set in 12/16pt Espinosa Nova Pro.

Typeset by JVR Creative India
Edited by Djinn von Noorden
Cover design by New Island Books
Cover image by Liz Kirwan
Printed by FINIDR, Czech Republic, finidr.com

New Island received financial assistance from The Arts Council (An Chomhairle Ealaíon), Dublin, Ireland.

New Island Books is a member of Publishing Ireland.

10 9 8 7 6 5 4 3 2 1

For Liz

I woke up this morning with a awful aching head
I woke up this morning with a awful aching head
My new man had left me just a room and a empty bed

Bessie Smith, 'Empty Bed Blues'

A woman comes to your door, a woman of about twenty-five or thirty and she hands you a set of keys. You are still trying to come to terms with the actual catastrophe and now this quiet, beautiful brunette passes steel and brass and walks away without a word. She could have put them through the letterbox. There are three keys and a plastic tag with a slot for the address. There is no address. Most likely the woman expected you to know it already. You watch her go down the street, something grossly animal twisting and turning under restraint in your throat. There are names you could call her but mostly it's just anger at the fact that she said nothing. And at yourself because you said nothing. Meekly you took the keys. Fifteen years, if your lower guess is correct, stand between you. You know she is his mistress, or rather his ex-mistress, the mistress of your ex-husband; you know it by some natural instinct for catastrophe that has only developed in you since the day you struggled against the bathroom door and found, after you had opened it a little, that you were pushing his body and judging by the lack of response of any kind, that he was dead or at least deeply unconscious and even more overweight than you had ever told him. Since then everything has been dangerous. You have not opened a letter without trembling. You let the phone go to the answering machine and listen to the voice for a few seconds before picking it up. Even now, you only answered the door after looking out from behind lace curtains.

1

This animus rising in my gorge. My eye is caught by a line of fine lace below the hem of her skirt. Tanned legs. I watch as she walks away. She has a deliberate pace, placing her feet one before the other almost in a line, which causes her body to remain completely upright. It projects intensity. I can't quite put my finger on what kind of intensity. She is slim, well built, well dressed and wearing expensive clothes. Her legs are first class. Her brown hair is rich and shoulder length. I remember that my own hair is brown and that only yesterday I found the very first grey hair. That once I had it cut to this same length. Did he ask me to do it? She turns the corner without looking back. Only then, when she is gone, do I realise what the stiffness and deliberateness means. The woman was frightened.

Mistress.

Fuck him. Fuck the dead body I put in the ground. Fuck the corpse inside the bathroom door. Fuck the heart that killed him not soon enough. I have been talking to myself since the day he died. And, in fact, maybe forever.

I slam the door so hard the doorbell rings. There's a loose wire, he said, I'll fix it.

Instead, he died of a heart attack while sitting on the toilet with his underpants down around his ankles and wearing his striped pyjama top. And his mobile phone. He used the mobile phone as a light. It was an Apple iPhone. Now mine. One of the first things I did after the funeral was change the SIM. It was news to me that I wanted it.

His frightened mistress. She was beautiful. She had brown eyes the colour of cherrywood.

As soon as the door is closed I think about the keys. Two flat Yale style, one a strange toothed steel shape like the key of a safe. I can't read the lettering. I get my glasses and go into the kitchen where the spotlights are bright. I am afraid. I tilt a key and read *CISA made in Italy* and on the other side *Costruz. Italiane Serrature Affini CISA*. The strange key has a plastic handle that says *Mottura* and the letter *E*. I sit down at the laptop and google *Mottura*. The second item in the search list: *Mottura Serrature di Sicurezza*: home. *Mottura Serrature di Sicurezza S.p.A. is the leader company in the production of europrofile security cylinders (Champions) ...* A quick glance at their home page shows that they make security locks for doors and locks for security safes. Aren't all locks and safes supposed to be secure? The *About Us* page tells me that they are based in Turin. I realise I am trembling. I went to Italy with him once. I remember him saying, I could get used to this. It was in a restaurant near the sea somewhere. On the west coast. We had taken a train journey from Nice. I remember the French side very well, the mountains, the little yellow stations, bougainvillea everywhere tumbling off houses and hillsides, the astonishing brittle sea between Villefranche and Èze-sur-Mer, the crowds getting on at Monaco, the enormous yachts, then the change as we crossed the Italian border, suddenly every inch of land a garden, fruit and vegetables and vines everywhere. We switched trains at Ventimiglia station, the first in Italy, and after that a blank.

An Italian door. Or an Italian safe.

Maybe that's where he put the money. I still cannot accept that all these years he was living off what was, in effect, a Ponzi scheme.

There must be a record somewhere in the chaos of his filing system. Down the hall, feet clattering on the parquet floor he insisted on, and up the stairs. Fear grips me as I climb back in misery. Hours, days, weeks of trying to piece together what my fate would be, must be, and how he set the clockwork going. When I open the office door there is an audible escape of air like a sigh, redolent of stale carpet, old plastic, paper and mould. This room regrets.

I see myself sitting in the disorder of his life, in front of his huge computer, entering unknown signifiers. I am the Rosetta Stone, an unbreakable code to myself, an alien way of being, an unknowable entity. I hate the self I see and see myself to hate.

My eye falls on the pile of letters. *We wish to inform you that we have a strict policy of pursuing all debts owed to us. Accordingly if payment is not made in respect of the above account within SEVEN (7) DAYS of the date of this letter we will be forced to instruct our solicitors to initiate legal proceedings to recover the debt owed by you.*

Not by me, by him. But him being dead it's me now. It's only me. Fuck debt and death together. Robbers both.

That was a letter about his car. Third and final demand. Then there were banks and other important institutions wishing to inform me that like me they hated his guts and now that he couldn't avoid them any longer through the simple fact of being six feet down in a fixed abode to wit a cemetery, they wanted their money back fast. There was that letter of Byron's, I forget to whom, in which he says that every guinea is a philosopher's stone, that Cash is Virtue.

These keys.

I think: does he have a safe deposit box somewhere in Italy? And if it's a safe deposit box, why the door keys? In Turin.

I turn from the computer and think about his filing cabinet. Yesterday I tried to make sense of the statements from five different banks. Even to my angry and unpractised eye the money had been haemorrhaging for two or three years. But last year he bought, or I thought he bought, a new Volvo. It had satellite navigation on a screen that emerged from the walnut-effect dashboard at the touch of a button. Heated front seats. He was like a child with a new toy except that he justified it by saying that you had to play big to win and that meant showing big too. I thought it was something he'd heard on *The Apprentice*, the only TV show he really watched anymore. I had never met anyone else who empathised with Alan Sugar and the board instead of the apprentices. He even called him Lord Sugar, and when he fired someone he nodded appreciatively. But the car was his mistress, his midlife extravaganza, his declaration of continued manhood. So I thought. Before I had reason to think otherwise. I thought it was pathetic but comfortable.

Three days ago I pressed EJECT on the stereo and Stan Getz came out. *Greatest Hits*. 'What's New?' 'Too Marvellous For Words'. 'You Stepped Out Of A Dream'. 'My Old Flame'. The great great Stan.

I open the drawers one by one. I take the files out and empty them onto the desk. Once I've checked through the documents I push them onto the floor and tip another file onto it. Eventually I come to a file labelled *Misc*. Even before I empty the contents my eye is caught by a piece of headed notepaper that says *Studio Notarile*. There is a logo that could be anything but certainly contains an arrow. I don't know what it means but it's Italian. I lay the file down on the desk and take the document up. I don't understand a word except to see his name on it. Then my eyes drift down the document and catch on some phrases: *Il possesso e il materiale godimento dell'immobile in contratto*. *Possesso* is maybe possessor or possession. *Immobile* is probably the same as *immeuble*, which means a building in French. *Contratto* must be a contract. There are several stamps on the page. I start to feed paragraphs and sentences into Google Translate. What comes out is a mess but I understand what it means. And the address is there: 112 Via Antonio Gramsci, Camogli 16032, Genova. I can find that. I google it and there it is on the map. My heart is thundering in my chest. A seaside village. I can see that there is a little harbour. The usual Italian street names, Mazzini, Repubblica, etc.

Mine now.

I just want you to know: I never loved you. You meant nothing to me.

Listen. I am talking to myself again. I sit looking out through the venetian blinds at the strips of reality that are visible. I see the roofs of cars parked across the road, the lower part of the first-floor windows, a strip of the roof and then lengths of grey January sky. I have to get out of here. Am I surprised by my own resolve? Shaken by the reality?

My plane comes in off the snow-bleached Alps and out over the sea, the wingtips shaking slightly in the turbulent crossing from earth to water. It takes my breath away. First all that intense white, the pointed ends of the earth, the valleys with their rivers or roads, too far away to see houses, something like mist or smoke, and then the cutaway coastline and the azure blue. The plane turns left and tracks along the coast then left again, turning tightly over a wooded promontory, then the descent and, passing under the wing, a scattering of small villages tilted to the sun, then a big low-rise city that must be Genoa. To judge by the angle of the flight, the airport is right on the sea.

I wait at the baggage carousel and watch as the luggage tips slowly out of the maw and goes a progress through the crowd and people take theirs and leave. I watch young couples with enormous hard plastic cases, an elderly Arab lady with two large black bags, an elegant Italian girl with what looks like a hat box, an American family with eight large suitcases and a ladybird case for their youngest to roll about on. Eventually the carousel is empty and my case has not come out. I wait until it stops, then I am directed to a desk that says *Oggetti smarriti*, which I assume means Lost Luggage. I report my single solitary grey suitcase. The woman behind the counter speaks English. She notes the details from the tag on my passport and enters them in a computer. The computer is slow. She tells me that the airline will telephone me when they locate the bag and it will be delivered to an address of my choice free of charge. I give her the address at Via Antonio Gramsci. An act of faith or hope. Normally these things take a day or two, no more, she says. She seems to think it is a minor matter. She looks bored then irritated. She raps her pen on the desk. I explain to her that I don't have as much as a change of underwear and she makes a sad face. It is a fake sad face. I would like to punch it. Then I am surprised that I feel like that. When did I begin to think of punching people? She explains to me that I am entitled to purchase clothes and any other necessaries and the airline is obliged to reimburse me within reason. She looks bored again. I think she is deliberately provoking me.

What does within reason mean, I say, I lost my clothes!

Any reasonable expenditure, she says. She gives me a receipt and wishes me a very good afternoon. Her pronunciation suggests she has studied in England. I want to ask her, but she has already turned away and is examining Facebook on her phone.

The arrivals area is empty now except for a man holding a sheet of A4 paper that says *Mr Landress*. He looks at me eagerly even though I am clearly not a Mr. I walk past him and out into the open air. I can see the taxi rank but there are no taxis. I guess that there isn't a flight due for some time. I stand there blinking in the brilliant sunshine, trying to think. Perhaps someone at the airport has a taxi number I can call.

I am about to go back inside when the man who was holding the *Mr Landress* sign stands beside me. Where are you going, *madame*, he says, perhaps I can help. But you will eventually see a taxi.

I tell him the address and he says his client seems to have missed his flight. He shows me the piece of A4 paper then crumples it and puts it in a bin that is attached to the taxi-rank sign.

Perhaps they mislaid him like my bag, I say, but the man does not understand. I have to explain that they lost my suitcase.

He shakes his head. We Italians are terrible, he says. There is no further explanation. I do not have the energy to tell him that the airline was British.

I can take you, he says. I live in the next city, it is a small detour, not much, a few kilometres, no more.

I ask how much and he says it would be nothing because he is going home, his client did not make the flight and his fare was prepaid by his company. I look around again, because I am not sure of getting into a car with a strange man. I remember reading an article about a woman in France who was kidnapped by a fake taxi driver. But this man does not look fake. So I decide to take a chance on him. I nod my head and he smiles and tells me to follow him.

He leads me along beside the building and into a sort of yard. There is only one car parked there and it is a Mercedes. The man holds the back door open for me and I get in, reassured that he didn't want me in the front seat beside him. The seats are leather. The feel and smell reminds me of the Volvo and my stomach contracts, a fist tight as a beechnut in my belly. I recall that I left the second demand letter on the desk with all the other stuff. The shit, as I had begun to think of it. He hadn't been paying bills for months. There were pending court cases. His solicitor, who had been my solicitor also, laid it all out for me. Then came the brown-eyed mistress with someone else's keys.

So yesterday, at eight on a crisp Irish morning, a sun that brightened without warming, the frost steaming on the roofs opposite, I booked my flights – first from Cork to London, then London into the unknown. Flight was the right word, I felt. I was fleeing rather than flying. I phoned my head of department and said I was taking leave and someone else would have to cover for me, I didn't give a fuck who, they could find someone or they could fire me it was all the one, I was leaving the country, and to be honest I couldn't get out fast enough. And before Claire could reply I hung up. The phone began to ring again almost immediately, although it had hardly rung at all since the funeral – creditors tend to write letters, or their lawyers do – and I simply took it off the hook, pressed the cradle and left the receiver on the desk. Then I packed the famous suitcase with the kind of clothes I thought people would wear in Italy in February, took the food in the fridge down to the Penny Dinners, though what they would do with my taste in canned sardines, baked beans, pâté and frozen prawns was anybody's guess. And this morning I drove his Volvo out to the airport. From the moment the tall thin man behind the counter in Penny Dinners took the Slazenger bag full of food from me, I felt weirdly weightless and unconstrained. The Slazenger bag was a leftover from the time we had both joined a tennis club. Somewhere there were tennis rackets too, and one of those little white skirts women are supposed to wear. I hated wearing it, not because I didn't have good legs, or because I didn't like miniskirts, but because it was so clearly a thing – a man thing.

These thoughts passed through my mind in a not entirely random fashion, not exactly a stream of consciousness, but in a relatively ordered set of reflections occasioned by the smell of leather seats. I have come to think of stream of consciousness as a mainly literary device not very well connected to the reality of what goes on in my head, contrary to the accepted view. Perhaps, I think, I am anal or repressed and maintain a kind of thought fascism.

The idea makes me smile. It is the first thought that has not been related to death, debt or dying that I can remember having since the moment I woke to a strange sound emanating from the en-suite. Later I rationalised it as the well-known death rattle, but at the time it just sounded odd. I lay abed for a few moments, possibly a minute or two, listening, aware that the other side of the bed was empty and that he must be in the bathroom, perhaps he was gargling, but ultimately it was the silence that got me up. If he were in the bathroom he should be showering, peeing, flushing, running a tap, shaving with his electric razor, blowing his nose or just moving around, and in fact he was doing nothing. In all our years together I had never known him to do nothing for longer than fifteen seconds. I got up, noting that his mobile phone was gone from the bedside locker, and pulled on my dressing gown.

The road rises above the city of Genoa and we are now travelling along a motorway hundreds of feet up. The driver's mobile phone, clipped to the dashboard, shows an intricate weave of crossed lines and the legend *Ponte Morandi*. Tunnels follow, bridges or viaducts and the glittering sea appears on my right whenever we are not underground. The driver is silent and the car is smooth and comfortable, if too hot. I could easily drift off. Last night I closed my eyes and was instantly asleep only to wake again forty minutes later, alert, restless, occasionally terrified, anxious. I revolved every scenario in my mind. I even saw the young woman naked in bed with him in some bright, cheap timeshare that smelled of fried fish. I had to sit up because the thought was a physical pain in my gut like a closing and unclosing fist squeezing whatever it was that was just below my midriff.

And this is me in the back seat of a car driving to where my ex-husband took his woman. I am looking out the window but in my eyes I see myself. A stranger.

I'm lost aren't I? I always was.

Now we are winding down into a valley, a modern town ahead, all concrete apartment blocks and shoddy factories. I'm smiling because it so exactly matches my lurid fantasy. There would be a street somewhere that had a tiny glimpse of water. That would be it. I wonder if there is a mortgage on the property. His solicitor never mentioned one when he informed me about the contents of the will and the pending debts. Perhaps he didn't know about the Italian connection.

But the car continues through the town, which I see is called Recco, and climbs a hill past a church and then the sea is on my right again and it is as blue as a baby's eye and little boats move over it like motes, and out on the horizon there is a ship that must be an oil tanker or a gas-ship and beyond that a cruise liner. And this town, I see, is called Camogli. The driver turns to me and jerks his thumb behind him.

Recco, this town we pass, he says, in 1943 the bombers came, before it was a – how do I say? – *medievale* town, after the bombers only three houses still there. He holds up his hand showing three fingers and repeats the word 'three'. American bombers, he said, because of the *ferrovia*, the bridge for the trains, they came at night, most bombs missed the bridge.

I look back over my shoulder, surprised that a concrete city should have such a long and tragic history, but the buildings are already long out of sight. There are contrails in the sky, snow tracks in the blue, two parallel and one at an angle of forty-five degrees, and a plane gliding down towards the airport, already so low I can almost see people behind the windows.

The mystery of the three keys is easily solved. The first key is for the gate, the second for the front door and the strange toothed one is for the door of the apartment. I know it is his apartment because his name is on the postbox at the gate and the number Two and here is the number Two in old brass beside an equally old brass doorbell. It is, I assume, a security lock.

Inside everything is dark. It takes me a full minute to realise that the shutters are closed. I press the home button on my phone to illuminate the screen and see the vague shapes of a table and chairs, kitchen cabinets in some dark colour, what looks like a coffee machine on a side table. I reach the window and open it and find the catch for the shutters, which turns out to be a heavy iron latch that lifts and swivels and squeaks and the shutters open and sunset floods the room. The amber light reveals a glass-topped table on iron legs, four kitsch chairs imitating antiques, a wine-coloured kitchen, a marble floor. It all looks expensive. Even kitsch costs.

There are double doors to my left, slightly ajar. I push them open and walk into a room with a big bookcase and two sofas, a little desk and chair under a window. I open the window and its shutter and see the sunset again, this time setting over the sea a hundred feet below.

A pine tree casts a slanting shadow. Then that familiar contraction below my midriff. On the desk is an A4 pad, a pen and a book called *What Is An Apparatus?*. It is held flat by two round black stones and certain words and phrases have been underlined. I read one aloud: *Apparatus, then, is first of all a machine that produces subjectifications, and only as such is it also a machine of governance.* I know for an absolute certainty that this book is not his, that he would not only not read such a sentence, but that he would not understand it, and that if he could understand it he would hate it intensely for the thought process that it implied. So she sat here, that beautiful young woman, with that pencil in her hand, gazing at this book and thinking about subjectification. She raised her eyes and looked out at this sea, this sunset or one exactly like it. What did she wear?

Suddenly I know what I will find.

I whirl about and march back through the double doors through another set of double doors and see a small bathroom and a bedroom to my left. The bed is unmade, just sheets twisted together, slightly stained. I know what the stains are. A large mirrored wardrobe on my left. I wrench the doors open and see dresses, blouses, jeans doubled over wooden hangers, a light puffy jacket. Some of his clothes too, a linen jacket such as he had never worn for me, would never wear, though I had tried to make him buy one on some forgotten French holiday. His usual shirts, but with short sleeves. Behind the next door there were drawers, one of which holds a plastic box containing her panties and his boxers jumbled together. Another, socks and tights.

I see it all through a mist of anger. I sit down hard on the bed, holding my belly, rocking, moaning in pain. I swear repeatedly.

Fucking shitting fucker fucking fucking bastard.

More. I don't even hear myself. I do not cry. Rocking, twisting, stamping feet, swearing, kicking, but no crying. Pain without tears.

I go into the bathroom and open the bathroom cabinet. I sweep her make-up, her moisturiser, her perfume, her mascara and all the other stuff onto the marble floor. A jar shatters and I stamp the glass into pieces. Then I have to remove a piece of glass from the rubber sole. I sit on the toilet and pick it out. I can smell Poison. I recognise it because it's what he bought me for Christmas. My head fills with a scent that is mine and not mine. Before driving to the airport this morning I dabbed some on my neck and wrists. Now the whole world is full of it.

I tread my way through the glass and stand in the kitchen.

I would like to smash everything but this is where I live now.

I start searching for a brush and shovel.

Time passes. I realise all the lights in the apartment are on. Did I turn them on? When I switch some off I am confronted by the solid wall of darkness beyond the glass. I'm hungry. In a kitchen press I find two bottles of wine. I search for a corkscrew and find it in a draining tray above the sink. All the cutlery is there. Four big wine glasses. It is called Nebbiolo delle Langhe. I've never heard of it but it tastes good. It must have been her taste, because he was more of an expert on beer. A packet of salted nuts while I drink and look for food. *On the lower shelf five vertical breakfast plates, six horizontal breakfast saucers on which rested inverted breakfast cups, a moustachecup, uninverted, and saucer of Crown Derby, four white goldrimmed eggcups, an open shammy purse displaying coins, mostly copper, and a phial of aromatic (violet) comfits.* That was Bloom checking his kitchen presses after Molly's lover Blazes Boylan had left. Bloom also betrayed but betrayer too. Boylan drank the bottle of William Gilbey & Son's invalid port. The indignity of it.

Did she know Joyce too? A joke between them, the mistress and the husband? Maybe she even attended my classes. I don't know her name and I'm not good with faces. How did they meet? And where?

There are packets of pasta, jars of sauce, herbs, spices, sugar, salt on the upper shelves. On the lower shelf only plain glasses and cups, no Crown Derby. I cook spaghetti and a sauce of some kind and drink steadily as I eat. The apartment, which was warmed by the sun, is cooling rapidly and the alcohol insulates me, but weariness overtakes before I finish the bottle. I find a duvet carefully rolled in the top of the wardrobe and throw it on the bed and crawl into the sex-stained sheets. I don't care. My head spins when I move and when I am at rest the room spins around me instead. What if? I fall asleep and dream. Recently I have been dreaming about childhood.

I wake with a start. My phone tells me it is four in the morning. Irish time, It feels as if someone has tied a hundred elastic bands round my head. The pain and pressure. My eyes forced into my skull by two huge thumbs. A dry mouth and cold to the bone. The crazy birds are already singing outside my window. I cannot find bottled water and I don't know if the water from the tap is drinkable. I drink it anyway. If I get some terrible parasitic disease it may kill me and that will cure this headache. There are no painkillers in the house. I try every cupboard in the kitchen and bathroom. Did the bitch never feel pain? And did he never feel pain in this secret place? Only at home and especially at that last minute sitting on the toilet wondering about indigestion? An undignified death.

I go and sit at the desk looking out the window. The shutters are still open and I can see the lights of a ship and maybe some fishing boats. It is a calm, cool night with stars. My head still feels as if it is moving when it isn't. How unfair, I think, to be drunk and also hungover.

The thought comes to me that they will find this house and sell it with everything else. They will find his car in the airport car park and sell it. They will empty his bank accounts, wherever they are. I suspect there are many. They will sell my home of twenty years.

And then it occurs to me that I didn't know about this place and neither did his solicitor. There is no evidence in any of his accounts of payments for it. Perhaps he was successful at this one thing.

Secrecy.

'Empty Bed Blues'. Bessie Smith. *I woke up this morning with a awwww-ful aching head.* The sexual throatiness, the grinding brass in the background. Bessie cranking it out. *I woke up this morning with a awwwww-ful aching head, my new man had left me just a room and a empty bed.*

There must be central heating. My feet are cold; the marble floor has cooled them. Is there a neuropathology that connects a pain in the head to cold feet? Why do we shiver in pain? I look around the flat and find a remote control with a digital display behind a vase on a side table in the sitting room. It is identical to the one I have at home. He didn't like change, or at least not where objects were concerned. Apart from sex objects, of course. I flick the cover of the remote control open and turn the heating on. I set the temperature at twenty-three degrees and hear a small pop as the gas ignites. Where is the boiler? Something to investigate later. The radiators in the room begin to tick. The ticking is the only sound inside the house. Outside there are the birds and the ships and fishermen as remote as stars.

I go into the bedroom and search in the box of socks and find a pair that fits. They say *Happy Socks* on the side. They are pink. I have always despised women who wear pink. I have warm socks in my suitcase but my suitcase is *en route* somewhere in the air or on the ground. Thousands of suitcases go missing every day, the woman said, and the majority are returned to their owners within a day or two. It strikes me that the air is full of people, all sitting in the same position, reading, sleeping, talking, eating, transporting other people's suitcases. If I could make the fabric of the plane vanish they would look ridiculous at thirty thousand feet.

A warm sweater. I put it on and immediately detect the faint trace of Poison. I don't care. I want the pain to stop. I am still unstable when I bend down, my head still turning. I go to the kitchen and pick up the bottle of Nebbiolo and bring it to the desk. I look at it and see about a quarter remains. What have I come to?

I drink from the bottle. Three deep swallows and I can feel the headache receding slightly. Tomorrow I will buy painkillers and make a fresh start. I will never do this again.

I go to the wardrobe and try on a pair of jeans. They fit very well. It makes me smile. I haven't lost my figure. I pull on the puffy jacket over the sweater, find the keys and go out. The label on the arm of the jacket says *Save The Duck*. I never knew the duck needed saving.

At the gate I don't know which way to turn.

The road runs down to the right and around a curve. I turn against the hill, cross the road and start walking. Almost immediately I am presented with a stairway leading down. At that moment, for no apparent reason, the streetlights go out. At the same time I hear a fast car coming from behind. The headlights pick me out briefly and fling my shadow against the wall and then it is gone. I watch the lights swinging on some tortuous road ahead and disappearing. The noise of a high-revving engine going away into the distance. My heart is racing. Inexplicably, I feel as if I have narrowly escaped death. The road is not for me.

I try to see down into the darkness. I see a railway line, a bridge, the steps continuing behind some buildings. Where do the steps lead? Wherever else, they will take me to the sea.

I go down step by step into the dark, the pain slowly turning into a dull ache between my eyes. I realise that my fists are clenched. I am afraid, but of what? This empty stairway? Everyone else is asleep. I cross the railway bridge and, as I do, a train comes out of a tunnel somewhere in the darkness on my left. The noise shocks and pierces and I clap my hands over my ears until the last carriage passes. Who is travelling so early or so late?

Where are they bound? Will the world they left be the same when they return? Or will some casual betrayal leave them untethered in the submarine cold of grief or anger? The wire fence is high. To prevent jumpers of course. In the slightest of shadows is contained a zone of the most profound darkness. Where is the line between light and non-light? Like, years ago, when I descended into the great cave and the guide turned out the lights and I and thirty or so studiously professorial academics were shocked into silence by the absolute absence of future.

If I could jump now.

A truncated life. She died, poor thing, weighed down by debt. But that quietus is not available to me thanks to a barrier and a sign that says *Non toccare, pericolo di morte*. No translation needed. And anyway, though I feel the fierce gripe of my own nameless dread, I know I am not that sort of person and mine is not that sort of fear.

I continue across the bridge and turn left down the shallow steps on the other side, then right again on a steeper, uneven stairs that leads to a little piazza the boundaries of which, as I pass through it, are suddenly etched by a rising moon on the gable wall of a tall house. Then more steps until I find myself in a tiny, silent port enclosed on all sides, tall houses at my back and left and right, and a steep stone mole on the seaward side, the entrance somewhere out of sight. The boats rest against their cables, fishing boats and pleasure boats all jumbled together. That smell of stale fish from a working harbour. There is not the slightest movement. The church stands behind the port. I count the floors on the houses. Some have six, some seven, even eight. I sit on a bench and breathe the salt air. Behind my head is a plaque with an inscription in Italian. It means nothing to me except that I recognise the words for sea, time and world. *Mare, tempo, mondo*. At the end of the long breakwater on the far side a tiny lighthouse. A single white flash every three seconds. The character of the light, my father told me. His father had been a light keeper.

The sign for a small hotel on my right. The lights are all out.

Perhaps it is the alcohol and the receding pain, but I feel suddenly tranquil here. These past weeks of hounding despair that was always at my heels, the stupidity of burial rituals (why couldn't I just stick the fucker in the ground somewhere?), the law, the Church (at least I drove the priest from my door – he may have been a Catholic, father, but I'm not, and he's dead so I make the decisions ...), his friends, the club, the registry.

The buildings here are ancient, streets and stairs worn down by the soles of the ages. How many deaths, bankruptcies, betrayals? And the church on its almost-island, joined to the world by two stone arches.

Sea, time, world.

How long does it take to learn a new language? And when will my suitcase come back?

The lights are on in a café as I go back. I have money. When I pulled on her jeans I felt the crinkling notes, two fives. That will certainly buy a coffee. The owner is putting ashtrays on the outside tables. He greets me with a warm smile and says *certo* when I ask for an espresso.

I watch the lights go on along the distant coast and he brings me the tiny cup and saucer. He hums while he works and I sip and feel warmed by the human contact. I am not entirely alone. There are always others. The coffee costs me a euro. He gives me the change with the same warm smile.

When I get home I search again and find a packet of tramadol in a drawer in the right-hand side night table with some other things of a feminine nature.

So now I know which side of the bed she slept on.

I pick up the pillow and sniff and think I can detect the slightest hint of woman. The heating has done a good job. I get in on the other side and then change my mind and slide across and lie on the faintly perfumed pillow. I close my eyes and am instantly asleep.

I am bleeding and my panties are bloodied. There are blood smears on the sheets. My pads are in my suitcase somewhere in the air. I find fresh panties in the box, ones that aren't too lacy or too small, and search in the bedside drawer on her side and find the packet of pads that I noticed last night when I found the tramadol. I go to the bathroom and turn on the shower. When the water heats I stand under it and let it pour onto my neck. The pain is still there. I stand a long time in the shower. I lose track of time.

I feel tidier then. I notice a trail of tiny blood spots. I unroll a chunk of toilet paper and follow them into the bedroom, cleaning as I go. Does marble stain? If I ignored them would there be a permanent pathway of rosy splashes? I go to put on the jeans and notice that they too are slightly stained. I must have been properly drunk last night. I find another pair and a T-shirt and then the heavy sweater. There must be a washing machine.

The thought occurs to me that when I came the electricity, water and gas were all working. He must have been due to come here soon, or he must have been here recently. Or she was here. I can almost smell her, a rank musk smell.

On my way into the kitchen I notice a router and a telephone on a tiny table. The router is glowing green. I pick it up and see the password and automatically enter it in my phone. Almost immediately there is a flood of emails with demanding subject lines: *Where are you? Your lecture today? Please respond: urgent. Are you OK? Urgent: Reply letter AIB Bank. Urgent: Final demand.* I had forgotten to switch to roaming and now I find myself wishing I had thrown the phone away before getting on the plane. Some are from his solicitor, some from my department, some from companies, creditors, some just spam. I notice that Mrs Aisha Ghaddafi is still addressing me as Dearest One and offering to cut me in on her late husband's secret millions. I almost feel affection for whoever the scammer is. I should write back: *Dearest Aisha, You are the only one who still believes in me ...*

I go into my settings and disable my email account. The notifications vanish. Then I look around the kitchen properly. There is indeed a coffee machine, I am relieved to see that I hadn't hallucinated it, an elegant red DeLonghi. I find coffee in the fridge — he always kept his coffee cold to preserve the flavour. Naturally there is no milk. Another bottle of wine, the same Nebbiolo, careful as always, when he liked something he kept buying it. I see no beer. A change of woman and a change of taste. And more spaghetti and sauce. I pack the coffee filter and make a strong double espresso and drink it quickly, then another, and another. Time passes at the coffee machine. I am feeding an old habit, drop by drop. When I look up there is light in the window. Daytime in Italy, a pewter and blue sky, light on the houses higher up the hill, the pale leaves of the olives, walls of ochre and lime and caramel and cyan. It makes me happy.

If one has to run away from one's responsibilities ...

I notice that I have almost run out of coffee. How many cups? I am feeling better. I take a tramadol, for my belly now as much as for my head, for the little convulsions by which I expel yet another egg of my already limited supply together with the lining of the womb that would have fed it. I have no children. I am forty years of age and it is still not too late. A line from Shakespeare enters my head: *We have ta'en too little care of this.* How long since I had to teach Shakespeare? But on the contrary I agonised for years about children. That, in fact, was the problem. Too much thinking allowed me to postpone the day. There is a Shakespearian play for every human eventuality; as regards babies, I am more Hamlet the over-thinker than heedless Lear. I had seen what happened to colleagues with babies. In those days it was simple: other people got promoted. And then, I was never sure that I wanted one. All that trouble, the sharing, the messiness of life with a child, a twenty-year commitment at the very least. If I had had one I would not be here. I would be drowning in debt and dread and worried about whether my child had a future. I might still drown but I will be alone. I have the feeling there is no escape. Ultimately there *is* no escape.

My heart is racing. This might become unpleasant.

In cases where a person dies from a natural illness or disease for which the deceased was not being treated by a doctor within one month prior to death a post-mortem may be ordered by the coroner. Findings: almost total closure of the arteries. A bomb in the heart. Steaks, cigars and Guinness. *We have ta'en too little care of this.*

Take physic pomp is the next line. Physic might actually have saved him. If he had taken a little more care.

Now I'm hungry and there is nothing to eat.

I go to the bedroom and pick up the puffy jacket. I examine myself in the mirror. I look good in her sweater and jeans. I think about Poison but decide against it. I pick up the keys.

I am about to open the door when the bell rings. For a moment I think he's back, he has followed me, come back from the dead, Hi, I'm Lazarus, I'll tell you all. Then I think it must be the girl because he's in a hole in the ground in Ireland and he's not getting out before Gabriel sounds his horn. The bell rings again. I stare at the door. The keys are in the lock. When the bell rings a third time, a shorter ring, hesitant, I catch the keys and turn them and the door opens. A tall, dark-haired woman is standing outside smiling. Her eyes open wide in shock and then cloud quickly. She says something in Italian of which I catch only the word *scusi*. She steps back and makes a small wave. Michela, she says, pointing to herself. Before I can say Kathleen she turns and moves away along the hall. The big main door, a battered, ancient piece of oak and brass, peeling and cracked and rotting at one corner, two and a half metres tall. I watch her as she goes out. I too step outside, closing my own door, walking to the front door, opening it, stepping through into the crisp sunlight, closing the door behind.

My own door.

Each movement feels both important and painful. This is my everyday now. This is my now and my tomorrow. The woman is going through the big cast-iron gate onto the road. She looks back again as she closes it and hesitates. She leaves the gate open and smiles. I am grateful for the smile. Then she is gone. Michela. I must make an effort to remember names.

In the supermarket I buy milk, yoghurt, muesli, tins of various kinds. No wine. I pay with my card because I want to keep my cash. What if they close my account? Or block it? Slam the door in my face? I should clean out the account as fast as possible. I go to the bank and withdraw my maximum, which turns out to be five hundred euro. Tomorrow I will do the same. I walk down the hill to a little café. This time on the main street. The light marks the shape of the buildings underfoot, I walk their ridge-tiles like a shadow of myself.

The price list is on the wall behind the counter and at least I know how to pronounce cappuccino. I point at what looks like a croissant and the woman behind the counter says brioche. Inspired by the familiar word I try my French on her but she just smiles and shrugs. She indicates a seat. An elderly man and an elderly woman, seated with their backs to the wall: the only remaining space is between them. The man has a glass of white wine and the woman has an espresso cup. I point to the outside and the woman takes the croissant/brioche from its glass case and hands it to me wrapped in a little paper napkin. She smiles again and turns to her coffee machine. I eat the croissant hungrily though it tastes nothing like a croissant. I detect the absence of butter. In addition it is partially filled with some sort of jam. It is an abomination, I think, but it is food. By the time the woman comes with my coffee I have finished it and I point to the empty napkin and somehow convey the impression that I would like a second one.

My phone begins to ring. It is his solicitor. I cancel the call. It rings again immediately and I cancel it a second time. When it rings a third time I switch it to silent and let it ring out. Then I switch the phone to airplane mode. I put the phone in my pocket. In her pocket really; the bitch's puffy jacket is as light as a feather. I wonder if she came here for her coffee? I am certain I can smell her perfume from the collar. Why did I never smell another woman on him? There were times when he worked late, when he came home and showered first, crawled into bed and was instantly asleep. Everyone knows I should be suspicious in those circumstances. I simply adjusted myself in the bed and slept the sleep of the just. And if I had suspected, what then? Confrontation, denial or admission, crisis. I hated crises. The irony of it.

I pay the lady and take the steps down beside the café. They plunge between looming buildings, old stone steps and swollen rust-red walls, and again the light, a brilliance that simply could not be home. A right-hand turn halfway down reveals the sea gleaming pale grey and silver under a thin layer of cloud. I emerge at the bottom on a promenade with shops and bars on one side and a low concrete balustrade on the seaward side, punctuated here and there by little squares and seating areas built out on the roofs of beachside buildings. A tiny bin lorry is making its way down the street. A bookshop with a stall outside. The children's books attract me; I wonder if I could send one to my nephews. The owner smiles from the doorway. Is this the most beautiful location in the world for a bookshop?

I buy an Italian phrase book with a basic grammar at the back. A Berlitz because Joyce taught at the Berlitz school in Trieste and Joyce is my passion and my profession. I describe myself as a teacher of Joyce, though in truth I teach modernism, which perforce includes lesser mortals. Did he speak Italian before he went? Yes he did, because on his first day in Trieste he got arrested for attempting to mediate between fighting sailors and was taken for a participant. He left Nora at the station while he was searching for a flat and then she discovered he was in gaol. But at the end he spoke the Triestine dialect better than Italian. How long does it take to learn a new language? When I learned French it was in school. There were years of it.

The hill leads down towards the old church and, I guess, the port where I sat last night. The church clock reads ten twenty-five. My phone is still on Irish time. Probably my metabolism too. The café at the bottom of the hill where I had that first espresso is called La Cage Aux Folles. I remember the film. Édouard Molinaro directed, 1978. *Combien de mamans a votre fils?* It makes me smile. I wonder if they serve lunch.

I feel a lightness and an opening out. I take a deep breath and then another. *He laughed to free his mind from his mind's bondage.* Joyce. What preceded it? *The note of banishment, banishment from the heart, banishment from home, sounds uninterruptedly from* The Two Gentlemen of Verona *onward till Fausto breaks his staff, buries it certain fathoms in the earth and drowns his book.* Old J.J. was fond of his own banishment, and here I am now, banished from the old sow, the old sod. I could reimagine myself as an exile, full of self-pity, a mournful spectre in the Italian sun, but what I feel is the opposite, as though I have found a real home or at least a hideout.

There is no breeze and the air is bright and fresh but not cold. I sit on a bench and turn my phone on again. There are eleven missed calls, all from his solicitor, or more probably from his solicitor's secretary. I open my phone contacts, find his name, scroll down the page and select Block This Caller. Small acts of resistance. It gives me a sense of satisfaction out of all proportion.

How many days and nights here? It already seems a lot. I try to count the number of times I have lain down in their bed. The scent is fading or I am becoming habituated to it. Some nights I bury my face in the fabric and long to smell her poison. It means I won in the end, that she's fading out, or some sensory gate is closing her out. I'm over it, I think, or almost. Or perhaps I am falling in love with the smell of her, the shadow of a body that he loved.

The brittle morning sunshine draws me out. I lock my door and turn to go.

An elderly woman, *una vecchia, una anziana.* My Berlitz serves me well as long as it's all in my head. I read, I understand, I do not speak. She stands in the hallway as I open my door. She seems frozen in the act of walking, one foot tilted onto the toe of a sensible leather shoe like an Oxford brogue. She swivels stiffly, marionette in life, all bone and no flesh, and greets me in Italian. Her voice is remarkably strong and deep. I shake my head and make that inane grimace that passes for an admission of my linguistic poverty. The usual pantomime begins. Italian? No. German? No. French? Yes. She begins to speak in what sounds to me like perfect, unaccented French. I answer competently, at least I think so. I have the feeling that she lived in France at some point, she has that flow that only total immersion can bring. As the sentences come, they bring others and I feel my fluency returning. I remind myself that I am not an idiot and that the linguistic structures persist in the interstices of the neural stairs and pathways.

She wants to know where I am from? If I am on holidays? If I am renting the apartment? What happened to the Irish couple that used to come there? What is my name? I answer each question in the list as best I can except for the one about the Irish couple. I tell her my name is Kathleen Holohan, Kathleen, but everyone calls me Kate. I tell her I too am Irish and immediately she switches to English. Her English has a slight Italian twist to it.

Can you take my arm? she says abruptly. It will help me down the steps. My name is Rossana Ferrara, please call me Anna.

Then as I walk her through the door and down the steps to the gate: do I like opera? What is my favourite opera? Do I like the Italians – Verdi, Puccini and so on? Mozart of course! What about Brecht? Do I have a driver's licence? In that case I can come to the opera with her. They are doing *Don Giovanni*. You drive and I will buy the tickets. I have a car, it's in a box just down the road. And afterwards we can eat out Roman style, or Dutch style as you say. It will be in the afternoon because I fall asleep in the evening. What do I do for a living? A lecturer in what? Oh she loves Irish literature. James Joyce of course. And Yeats even though he was an old fascist, he still was something, no? Beckett so dark but such a master. Can you walk me across the road, we drive so fast here? Italians are crazy. This is my Cadillac (pointing at a three-wheeled mobility scooter). Thank you, I'll just sit here while I catch my breathing.

Catch my breath, I say, regretting it immediately. But she laughs. Yes, of course, catch my breath. I'm going down to sit looking at the sea. I can drive right down to the mole at the back of the church. Isn't this the most beautiful place in the world?

I haven't really looked at it. As I say it I realise it's true.

Why not? It's beautiful, like a postcard. People come here just to make photographs of the sunset.

Yes the sunsets are beautiful, I say, trying to remember if I've seen one.

She swings her feet onto her scooter. You like it? My chariot of fire. Electricity is a kind of fire, I think. It's English. If you could take the thing out of the wall, what do you call it?

The plug?

The plug, yes. Thank you. Put it into this basket here. Now I am going to drive away. Thank you ever so much. I shall send you a note about the opera. What am I saying, we are house neighbours. I shall knock on your door.

Please do.

She moves out slowly and almost silently onto the road and drives off. As she rounds the bend she waves without turning round. I feel caught up in her rackety energy like a scrap of fabric lifting in a sudden breeze. What an astonishing person.

A small, grey-blue, three-wheeled lorry passes going the other way and the driver waves too. It sounds more like a motorbike in a tin box. All this waving. I almost feel local.

I go down the steps, across the bridge, down in the shade of the high buildings. I turn onto the main street and see a banner in bold red writing that says *San Valentino – Innamorati a Camogli.* A poster on a pole underneath says *Festival of the Lovers.* Taken aback, I check my phone and it is indeed February the fourteenth. There are heart-shaped cakes in the bakery, a wall of love-poems under the old arch, plates with a pair of lovers in a heart in the window of the kitchen shop, an evening dress in the clothes shop with a heart-shaped section in lace sweeping down in a curve to the cleavage.

Did he come here for the festival of lovers? I have a vague memory of getting a text for Valentine's Day a few years ago, something he never remembered. He may have been reminded in the office or he may have been abroad, I can't remember. It was the first and only Valentine's text I ever got from him. What did she wear for the festival of lovers, his bitch, did she wear this coat, these jeans, these panties and bra?

The day darkens, a lowering grey sky, a hint of rain or at least the humidity is high. The pathetic fallacy. On the mountain someone is burning clippings and the smoke drifts down over the town – I can see his fire on the wooded ridge beyond the old church. What do they burn in February? October days in Ireland, the first kindling catching in the chimney, the crackle. I reach for that sensual comfort as a child reaches for a beloved toy. But it cannot protect me against the festival of lovers.

That familiar tourniquet, the tightening screw, my breathing shortening. An empty bench presents itself and I sit. Nobody knows I am wearing his mistress's clothes. I stare, dry-eyed, in an agony of jealousy and anger and lonesomeness at a piece of graffiti that very slowly resolves itself into words: *Non è mai troppo tardi farsi un' infanzia felice*. I have to concentrate to work it out though it should not be hard. *Infanzia felice* is the key. Both words have cognates in English. Infancy. Felicitous. *Tardi* equals tardy. It's not too late to make a happy childhood, or words to that effect. I laugh so hard that a passing couple stops to enquire if I'm okay. They try it first in German, then Italian and finally English.

Yes, thank you, I say, I was just laughing at that wall.

And I point at the graffiti. They look. And they too laugh.

You have a good weekend, they say, their English pitch-perfect New York-style American movie. You have a good weekend. And they move on.

I buy my milk and my focaccia and walk home by the sea. The only other stroller in the little port is a woman with a chihuahua in a tweed coat in a child's pram. A single sailing boat crawls over a pale grey ocean. It must be fucking cold out there. Shutters are set at half open. From one window, slightly ajar, a saxophone solo. I stop and listen. Stan Getz, 'Autumn Leaves'. The past.

At midnight the phone rings. I struggle out of sleep, out of a happy dream of escape, I am alone in a boat on a tranquil ocean, the movement comforts me like some dream of belonging. I rise out of the depths reluctantly. It is my sister and I am immediately alert to danger. I can hear a television in the background. I imagine her seated on her leather reclining couch idly watching whatever game show Gerry was watching. Or *Strictly*. What time is it at home? When is *Strictly* on? Home is an hour behind, so eleven o'clock there. The telephone to her left ear, a glass of wine in her right hand.

Where are you? she says.

I'm out of the country.

Where?

It's none of your business. I'm on holiday.

You're bankrupt, for God's sake. You can't just go on holidays. Do you have any idea how worried we are?

I hold my breath, then exhale slowly and, I hope, silently. Big sister. The things I have escaped. A childhood of hectoring, bullying, spitefulness and jealousy. Not all on her part. Families are complicated and corrosive mechanisms. They eat each other.

When she begins again I can hear her exasperation, her temper rising.

Gerry was talking to Mick Cussen today and he said you're not returning his calls or answering emails. He's worried about you. He can't progress your problem without you signing stuff. You have to go in to his office. I'm worried about you myself. You can imagine we thought the worst.

Another long silence. Then I say, they're not my debts, Alice. I didn't spend that money and I didn't borrow it. I didn't even know he was borrowing it. They can work it out between them. I refuse to be involved.

Don't be stupid. You are involved. You had your beautiful house, your clothes, your holidays. You partied too.

I had my salary. I'm a public servant.

My sister laughs. Your salary!

In case it escaped your notice, I work for a living. I always have.

If you can call it work, she says.

At that point, infuriated by her tone, I hang up. Gerry is an accountant. I don't know how much money he makes but I am certain it is a lot. In any case his opinion of public servants of any kind, and teachers in particular, is that they are parasites who depend on his hard-earned income tax to lead lives of idleness. My ex-husband usually agreed. Loyalty was not one of his strong points. In fact, clearly, it was not one of his points at all.

For the second time since I came here I walk out into the empty night. I turn right at the gate this time and walk along the silent road. High up in one of the houses, maybe four floors above, I hear a baby's sudden cry and the hushed voice of a father. A baby is born, a being, a living heart, brain, voice, expresses himself or herself in the present, later in the other tenses and moods, the past, the future, the conditional. But the first universal assertion is that barbaric yawp over the rooftops of the world. The verb to be, *être*, *essere*. I am. I am here. Feed me. Why is the one verb that casually asserts our existence so often irregular? I am, you are, he is. *Je suis, tu es, il est. Sono sei, è.* My grammar book confirms that our existence is so uncertain or so complex that the verb we use to express it must cavort manically between forms and even roots. I see that in Italian it goes from *è* (he is) in the present, to *fu* in the remote past. I think of Heidegger on Aristotle: *He was born, he thought, he died, all the rest is anecdote.* Such are our lives. They live more in the mouths of others for however short a time, with more certainty and more grace, than in our own heads or hearts. Time tells us while we cannot tell time.

There is a pathway with an iron railing on both sides. I follow it down to a crossroads. On my left-hand side, picked out by the streetlight, a tiny triangular garden with a huge mimosa tree, the acid yellow flowers gleaming in the moonlight, profuse and beautiful. The seeds are poison. And then, on a rocky ledge, a giant agave, big spiky tongues with cardinal red globes of flower. Now I am walking along a good pathway with the sea below. I come eventually to a little park among olive trees from which I can sit looking out at the lights of the coast and the ships coming and going to Genoa. I realise I still have my mobile phone in my hand. I look at it. There is one missed call.

I didn't even feel the vibration. My sister again. This is the pattern of my relationship and has been since childhood, a dance of approaching, confiding, fighting, parting and approaching again. My older sister. She became my mother when my mother left. All the strength and fragility of unsought duty. Impotent rages, casual slaps and hair-pulling. She became the cleaner to my father, the housekeeper, the cook until he found a woman to do it. And she assumed the responsibility of getting me to school on time, making me do my homework, making my bed. The trivia of childhood. I hated her for every single thing. I was wrong but I was a child. As children our hatred is stronger and more tenacious than our love. I would undo all that if I could.

Stupid unwelcome tears come again. I try to stop them at first, wiping them roughly with the flat of my hands, but soon I have wrapped my arms around my belly and I'm doubled up on the seat, rocking backwards and forwards and occasionally repeating the usual curses – bastard fucking fucking bastard, etc. After a while it stops. I can feel myself calming. It's almost as if I can see myself. Slowly I sit up and become aware of a man standing beside me. The shock almost starts me off again. But the man is elderly, completely unthreatening and wearing a white sailor's cap. He is low-sized and stocky and his hands hang loosely by his sides. He says something to me in Italian and I shake my head. He says something in German. I know it is German because I recognise the sound. Again I shake my head. English? he says hopefully. I nod. He lifts the little cap politely and then puts it back on his head at a jaunty angle. He winks and I smile.

I sit down? he asks. I gesture to the free space.

I come here, he says, because not sleep.

Me too.

We exchange smiles. He settles himself beside me and together we watch the sea and the night for a time. I want to leave but feel it would be discourteous and so I determine to pass an acceptable amount of time in his presence. But as the silence deepens I feel more comfortable. He moves around a lot, probably trying to make his skeleton comfortable on the hard timber of the bench, and makes small, involuntary noises as he does so. My father did that. I remember him shifting in his chair by the fire, a glass of whiskey on the table beside him. Paddy Flaherty would make a man out of a stick, he used to say. At one point I wonder if, in fact, the old sailor has fallen asleep, but when I steal a glance at him his face is set to the west and his eyes gaze intently or vacantly at the sea. I notice again the cap.

You are a sailor?

Long long time, he says. On *petroliere*. You say tanker? I was *macchinista*.

I nod my head. I have no idea what *macchinista* means.

He nods his head too and then the silence re-establishes itself. I wait perhaps five minutes and then cough and pull my coat up around my neck and say, Well goodnight, it was nice meeting you.

He looks at me and smiles and lifts his cap again. His face dissolves in a set of radiating lines like waves from a splash. The smile is irresistible and I smile back. My heart lifting a little – I feel it. I hold out my hand and he shakes it. Again the memory of my father, the seeming solidity of bone, the inflexibility, like little iron tubes wrapped in translucent flesh, a bag of bones, as he liked to say. And then I go home past the beautiful deadly mimosa, the sea of steady and winking lights, and the distant *sshh* as it falls on stones.

I have taken to leaving my door ajar. I hear the comings and goings, Michela with her camera, friends calling, Anna on her way to her chariot. When I hear her step I go out to greet her. More often than not I accompany her to the gate. Once and only once she objected. If I needed an aid, she said waspishly, I would have asked the *comune* to provide one for me. But mostly she is grateful for the arm to steady her pendulum swing from step to step and I for the human contact.

And this morning, having escorted Anna to her chariot on her way to see her doctor, I sit on a step in the sunshine and think about my life and how I lived it like a naive narrator in a trivial novel. I think again about my dead husband's hiding and veiling of himself. *Hiding and veiling* is Bacon, I think. That consummate discoverer of others' faults.

As far as I understand his treachery, he began by building a Ponzi scheme. When that began to unravel he tried to cover the losses by spread betting on borrowed money. The correct term, I discovered, was leveraged. He was leveraged up to his ears. And yet he had the money to live here.

He had the money to live here.

I go back inside and begin to search the house again, this time with more care. I am a scholar, I tell myself, I have spent a lifetime uncovering things, finding meaning. This is not impossible. I examine everything, take nothing at face value. A meticulous and invasive probe. I am driven by certainty. Everything about this second life of his, or this first life perhaps, demanded secrecy and subterfuge. I would find something. A safe perhaps.

Instead, in the little side table by the couch, I find a tiny, shallow drawer. It is almost a secret drawer because it has no handle. It is so obvious as to be banal. I notice it when I open the drawer above it and something else rattles. I put my hand underneath and slide it out by the pressure of my fingers. It contains a debit card for an Italian bank in his name. I stare at it for too long. *Shake and bend my soul*. Of course he kept that card here. He wouldn't risk it being found at home. There must be money if there is a debit card. I can feel my heart quickening. A chance to live a little longer in this place.

I take it to Piazza Schiaffino but the *bancomat* has a handwritten sign sellotaped to it which says *Guasto Broke* <=. So I go into the bank following the arrow. I am slightly panicked. My heart. I wonder if the stress of these weeks or months will shorten my life. I have to push a button to open the outside door, then step in and wait for the door to close behind. For a brief moment I am in a space the size of a largish vertical tomb walled with glass. Then the inner door opens and I go in. I look around and see that there is also a *bancomat* inside. I insert the card, wait while the screen shows *attendere prego*, then select English as my language. I choose *Balance in Account* and the machine demands a PIN. He only ever used two – the last four numbers of his mother's telephone number and his birthday. I start with the first. Wrong PIN. I try the second. Wrong PIN. Then I notice that there are six spaces. So I use his birthday and the year in full and it works. The relief is mixed with disappointment. Instead of secret thousands there are hundreds. This is an account for paying the domestic bills. Maybe there is another somewhere but I have no way of knowing.

Still. I found it.

I withdraw two hundred.

I'm stealing from *him* now.

But I am stealing from him what he hid from me – his secret home, his mistress's clothes, his money. The life he only partly lived. I laugh aloud and then blush as I catch a teller's eye.

His secret cache.

I leave. I have to push the button to open the inner door and then step inside the glass grave. I can smell Poison when the door closes. I turn to see who has come in, but no one else has entered the bank. So the smell is from me. I shrug. It doesn't matter anymore. The outer door opens and I step outside. It is raining. That is completely unexpected. I rush down the street as the rain turns to a downpour, the road already steaming and raindrops ricocheting everywhere, and duck into the café again. Three older women are sheltering there before me and parked under the awning is the mobility scooter. Inside I can hear the voice of Anna Ferrara somewhere behind the others.

She sees me immediately and calls me to sit beside her. Again the middle chair is free. In rapid Italian she tells the lady behind the counter about me; all I catch is the word *amica*. I am her friend, it seems. I know by the gestures and the looks that they're talking about me. Then the word *Irlandese*. The lady brings me a cappuccino even though I haven't asked for one. The remainder of the conversation, I assume, is mainly about the rain, which is battering the ground outside and hammering off the awning. I sit there in the steaming warmth and wonder what good fortune drew my attention to the shallow drawer with the card inside. How long will the money in his secret account last? Could it be that it is replenished at intervals from another secret hoard? I need to know how much time I have before the gas and electricity stop. Water too, perhaps.

The rain stops as suddenly as it began.

Her car is a surprise. It is a very old, yellow Volkswagen Beetle. The seats are ancient faded and cracked leather. The wheel is so heavy I wonder if I know how to drive anymore. The box she was referring to on that first morning when she took my arm and demanded I drive her to the opera is a garage among other garages buried deep inside the hill. She sent me down with precise instructions: first you press an electronic key and a gate in the rock slides back; then you walk down a long corridor and turn left and left again. By now I am a hundred feet into the rock. The 'boxes' are caged lock-ups. I peer through the fine mesh and see that some of them are empty and others are elaborately furnished. One of them is hung with paintings, another contains stacks of wine boxes and another contains what looks like the inside of a café complete with a giant Pavoni coffee maker and four tables.

A second electronic button opens the up-and-over door to Anna Ferrara's box, number seventeen. The car is in there, covered in a fine layer of dust. I am surprised to have to open it with a key and that the key physically opens a lock and a little Bakelite nib pops up inside the window. How have electronic keys, in the space of ten years or so, erased the physical memory of a lifetime? When I sit in I feel a rush of sensations that are really memories. The smell of the leather, of petrol, of something damp, I am in an uncle's car, coming home from school. Even then the car was a notorious and ancient wreck. He had two hunting dogs and they sat on the back seat and one of them licked my neck. I remember that the rack-and-pinion was faulty, despite having no idea of what a rack-and-pinion is, and the car would make unexpected darts across the central line, and sometimes towards the ditch, and my uncle would curse under his breath and wrestle with the steering.

The space feels cramped until I realise that I am sitting on the left-hand side, that my right hand moves the gear. I feel uncertain, almost unsafe, with only my left hand on the wheel. I turn the key in the ignition and the engine winds over a few times and then starts. Immediately the tiny box fills with smoke and fumes. I close the door fast and move the car out into the passageway. It jumps forward in three fast gulps and then the engine dies. I start up again and let the clutch out more slowly this time, revving the engine carefully. The car moves forward and I heave the wheel to the left. I am pleased to see that there is no steering problem. Does this model have a rack-and-pinion? Soon I am far enough away to stop, press the button to close the up-and-over door. I watch, as advised, to make sure the door closes properly. Then I put the car in first gear and let the clutch out again and the car crawls forward. In the confined space I don't dare move it into second.

I manage to make my way out onto the road, reminding myself that I must drive on the wrong side, and turn left and accelerate and slide the car up two gears. I drive along the coast road in third, conscious that everyone is turning to look at the noisy yellow blob going by. I am lucky that the tiny space in front of the gate, more a widening of the road than a parking space, is free and that the road is briefly empty. I drive in head first and then manoeuvre to get my tail in too. I ring Anna's doorbell and she comes out onto her balcony and waves. I wait by the gate and then, as time passes, I walk back and forward, and then I sit into the car. Eventually I hear the gate closing behind me. In the rear-view mirror, I see Michela helping Anna down the last step then waving goodbye. I rush around to open the passenger door. She wears a blue suit, sensible shoes and a mouthful of bright red lipstick, a gold locket her only ornament. She sits in, full of sighs and mutterings, panting slightly.

There was a time when I never thought about how to get into a car, she says, now I have to plan it like a battle. The body forgets.

She lifts her legs in, one by one, and rearranges her skirt and the skirts of her coat. Then a hand to her collar, closing it slightly, and an imperious wave with the other hand. I close the door.

Now my dear, she says, we will drive to San Rocco and have cocktails in the bar, which has the best sunset in the world.

She taps the dashboard. *On y va!*

I am wearing the bitch's sunglasses, another find. They had fallen down behind the hall-stand. Seeing the world through her shades. They are expensive – Maui Jim. I would never have paid so much.

I pull into the road, jerkily, nervously, reminding myself again of the right side /wrong side problem, and immediately there is a car behind so close I cannot see its bumper. Where did it come from? I could swear it wasn't there when I checked. A young woman watching me – impatiently I assume. I see her tap the flat of her hand against the wheel. I take a deep breath and concentrate on the road ahead. I have never driven on continental roads. How did that happen? Among the things I didn't notice in my life. The many.

I round the bend and head up the hill past the garden of olive trees and the old folks' home and then, on a straight but narrow stretch, the Italian car overtakes me, driving, in fact, on the side of the road on which I feel I belong. She leans in my direction as she passes and makes a circular gesture with her hand which I assume translates as, for God's sake, drive! Good riddance, I think. A sudden surge of emotion makes me want to follow her and tailgate her the way she did me. Somewhere inside still, lurking and ready to scratch and claw, is the Irish lecturer and wife of a secretive and deceiving husband, a fury in waiting, an imminent virago, a termagant, a harpy. The treasure of words in any language for a woman who won't take it lying down. I sense this repressed rage like an incubus. I wonder idly if it's possible to distance myself from my own personality. I have the feeling it would be regarded as an illness, that distance. Alienation, I think ruefully, how does one go about getting it? For perhaps ten seconds I would have driven that woman off the road and watched her tumble down the hillside through olives and orange trees to come to rest on the railway track below.

Instead I wind my steady way upwards through the narrow streets and country roads until I reach the level of Ruta. There, just after a sign that says that Nietzsche once lived here, Anna tells me to turn right and I find myself driving along the western side of the peninsula on the wrong side of the road.

What are you doing, she yells, this isn't an *autostrada! Merde!*

I swerve back to the correct side and laugh.

I liked when you said *merde*, I say.

Just stay on this side, she says with what I hope is mock bitterness.

Then she adds, My heart is not as it was.

I come to a sign that clearly means no cars beyond this point but she waves me on. Invalids, she says, can go anywhere and I am an invalid, no? Do I know the song of Jacques Brel? '*Les Vieux*'?

She begins to sing, a cracked thin voice, no longer able to hold the tune exactly, *Les vieux ne parlent plus, ou alors seulement, parfois du bout des yeux.* Do you know what it means? Of course, your French is excellent. I will teach you the words. Sing with me, no? *Les vieux ne parlent plus* ...

And so I drive carefully through the darkening chestnut woods to the little village singing in French with the old Italian lady in the yellow Volkswagen Beetle. And all the time, as I sing, I am conscious of the incongruity of life. These strange things. Only a few weeks ago I heard the noise in the bathroom.

By the time I reach the village I have learned the first verse.

Where did you learn your beautiful French, Anna?

A sly smile. Pillow talk, my dear.

Then the comedy of descending. *Scendere* is the Italian word, she tells me, for getting out of a car or descending stairs. She is too stiff to get out on her own and I have to give her my arm. She complains in Italian. Judging by the difficulty she has straightening, I guess her complaints are directed at her back. My father too, when he climbed out of the car, put his right hand to the small of his back as though to push himself upright. I prop her against the back window and go round locking each of the doors. She laughs. No one will steal this piece of German shit, she says. I hear the metal tumblers turning, the locks engaging. Cars are not like that anymore. It feels strangely alien, a physical and mechanical engagement with the machine that never happens in these days of microwaves and Bluetooth.

Then I take her arm again and after a time I find that she is moving more lightly, more loosely. By the time we reach the village there is a spring in her step. She is talking again. She tells me that she will teach me Italian because we cannot continue to converse in a pidgin of English and

French. The pidgin part is news to me – I was under the impression that my French was good. She has a dictionary of English and Italian that she can give me. It is a bit old and doesn't have computers and such things, but these are not essentials and the book will be perfectly good for what remains of life outside of technology. I want to say Not much, but I hold my tongue.

Then, passing the church of San Rocco she informs me that Rocco was the patron saint of lepers and people with the plague, not much called upon these days, and then, quite matter-of-factly, that the Pope, the land barons and the Bourbons ruined Italy, everybody blamed Cavour and so on, but Garibaldi was worse because he had a revolution and then he handed it all over to that stupid childish Victor Emmanuel, it was too much don't you think? At least he said he was a socialist, Garibaldi I mean of course, absolutely, even if he didn't know the meaning, and here is the bar, isn't it delightful? It's charming. Look!

She turns and sweeps her arm wide to indicate the bay hiding in its smoky evening, the lights of the houses along the darkening hills, the distant glow of Genoa and the ships in the roadstead, and the tranquil sea between. The sun is setting, red as a blood-orange behind the distant hills. It is breathtaking.

I feel like I have been caught up in a whirlwind and the leavings of history are swirling about as I ascend out of control. But I sit at a little table with my back to the bar and face the sunset and she orders two Negronis and nibbles. And she sighs deeply, contentedly, and for the first time she thanks me. What is the word, she says, for when someone steals a person?

Kidnap, I say.

Yes, she says, I think I have kidnapped you.

She cooks risotto in, she says, the Milanese style. She waves a little Tupperware container at me and I see that it contains chilli peppers. The classic, she says, has what do you call it? Parsley. But in Milan during the war we didn't have parsley because there was no outside, most people didn't even have gardens, so we used chilli pepper, don't listen to what people say, saffron and such things, this is the classic. Absolutely. I won't hear of anything else.

It's very good, I say.

Italian cooking, she says, is based on three ingredients – *olio, aglio e prezzemolo*, oil, garlic and parsley. You can turn anything into food with those three things.

Sounds very simple.

Simple food is the best. This is where the French are wrong. They think everything must be complicated.

My eye is drawn constantly to a photograph of a handsome man and woman standing very close, almost leaning against each other. The woman is very like Anna Ferrara. There are colourful boats in the background but they could be from any time, the same boats are moored, together with modern plastic tubs, in the harbour below. But the background is not this town, the little port, it's bigger and wider and more open. And something about the photograph suggests that the couple in it are not husband and wife or lovers. The man is dressed for summer in an open-necked shirt. He has a big head of hair, combed back from his face. His eyes express both sadness and humour, a big smile and a half-wink, deeply creased by something that cannot be age because he doesn't look more than forty. Fears or cares? A rough beard shadow. She is wearing a frock and a headscarf, sunglasses tilted back to reveal eyes that adore the man.

Is this you? I say, tentatively.

She swivels in her chair and looks at the photograph. She nods her head slowly. Yes, she says, that was me. A long time ago.

And the man ...?

A comrade.

She says no more. I am surprised by her choice of word but do not believe I can ask. Why not friend? Instead, I concentrate on my risotto and my wine. I praise the wine. She tells me it's just a simple Rosso Piceno, six euro from Leo down at the port, do I know Leo, he's charming, he consigns to the house.

Delivers? I suggest.

She looks at me for a moment. Yes, of course, delivers. And the grocers deliver. Everyone delivers to a woman of my age.

We sip our wine together and words come to me unbidden: *He smellsipped the cordial juice and, bidding his throat strongly to speed it, set his wineglass delicately down.* That's James Joyce, I say, Bloom drinking a glass of wine in Davy Byrne's pub in Dublin.

She laughs. Your Mr Joyce was a funny man.

Bloom was eating a gorgonzola sandwich with olives on the side.

Gorgonzola in Dublin in the time of Mr Bloom? I don't believe it.

Oh yes. A friend of mine published a paper on food in Joyce. Findlater's advertised it in their magazine *Lady of the House*. I remember their advertisement was *Cheddar, Gorgonzola and other varieties of Home and Colonial cheese etc. etc. Canadian pea-fed bacon a speciality*.

She laughs. How old was Bloom? A gorgonzola sandwich would keep me awake all night. It might even kill me.

I know the feeling.

Old age, she says. When I was young I considered old age to be an ideological failing. The Delphic oracle, you know, told Trophonius that the people who are beloved of the gods die young. That is what I thought. All young people think they are the favourites of the gods, no? I never expected to be old, what a shock, to wake up one morning and find I am still alive sixty years after I first read Greek. And then the years mount one on the other. But let me tell you, I regret nothing except that we did not win.

She gets up from the table, leaning with both hands on it, straightening slowly, and goes to the little kitchen and comes back with a bottle of straw-coloured liquid and two glasses on a tray. *Passito*, she says, sweet wine. The glasses jiggle together, faintly belling the arrival. Old age is full of useless energy, she says, look how my hands shake, like a girl in love.

She places the tray on the table and holds it there for a pause of three seconds. Then she sits down.

But I speak only of myself. Tell me about you.

I cough and blush and realise that the blush is something new and wonder if the change of life is upon me, and then I remember my period, and I wonder if these rambling, panicked thoughts in response to a simple question are also an effect of the change, or just stress, and then I notice that a time has passed, a minute maybe more. She has already poured the wine. She is looking with concern at my face. It must be showing consternation. I shake my head and determine not to be submerged by events. I actually say that.

I will not be submerged by events.

This statement elicits a slow, considered nod of the head and the word, almost whispered but with something like ferocity, *Brava*.

I take a deep breath and tell her everything. But I begin with the story of how I met him.

We were outside a disco at university, I tell her. Standing in a queue on a cold frosty November night. I was with a friend. I was excited by the idea of the dancing, the music. Behind us were two boys trying to make conversation.

Of course, she says, boys do that. They have an instinct for possessions.

At one point, as the queue shuffled forward, my friend whispered that one of them was a poet. She said it with a contemptuous twist. In English, as spoken in Ireland, the word poet can be said in one syllable, like coat. It can sound like contempt. But I was intrigued. I had never met a poet and I was already thinking of doing a master's in poetry. I thought I might learn something so, I suppose, I flirted with him. You know how it goes. Then in the opening of the doors to the disco and the press of the crowd I lost sight of him and it was almost an hour before I met him again. This time he asked me to dance and that was it. I danced one set and then spent an hour sitting with him between the broken lockers on the corridor outside. I remember the song that was playing as I kissed him for the first time was 'Leaving on a Jet Plane'. I remember that he loved Yeats and it was Yeats that I was planning to write my thesis on, though luckily I was dissuaded by the woman who would eventually become my supervisor. (Make it Joyce, she said, they're all bloody men, it's time we applied a feminist lens.) Part of our lovemaking was the swapping of quotations. It was ridiculous and romantic at the same time.

This is quite normal, she says. She is smiling. Love and poetry belong together, no?

I shake my head. If only.

I met your husband, she says, and he did not seem like a poet to me.

Yes, of course, she would have met him. And his mistress. The thought is a shock. I wonder about her ability to be blunt and warm at the same time. But I agree, by the time he came here he had already been a not-poet, an anti-poet for a very long time. Poetry didn't survive his first week at work. He decided that making a lot of money wasn't compatible with it. Or the other way round perhaps. He had the ability to blow with any wind.

So I tell her the story of the rest of my life in at most twenty sentences. I feel I should have kept count, used the skills of precis that my father was so keen on in my childhood. But it sounds like a tranquil idyll after a few glasses of wine: he worked and I taught. It was the perfect combination. We both travelled independently, I to conferences (I was never much of a holiday person but enjoyed the company of other academics) and he to whatever business people do when they meet. Playing golf seemed to be a large part of it. Business conferences often took place near golf courses, or sometimes even in them. I imagined him nipping smartly from hole to hole, an image not inconsistent with the reality, as it turns out. His movements were always busy rather than fast. Of course, I never suspected the hole he went for. He never talked about work or pleasure and after a certain point I didn't talk about books or poetry either. We died to each other in those years; unspoken became my afterlife.

But you loved him once?

Oh yes, I say, I think I loved him up until the end. In my own way.

And at the end?

I stand up and walk around the room. My pacing brings me to the photograph.

Who is this comrade, I say, pointing at it. A lover?

That, she says, was Enrico Berlinguer and I'm not sure but I don't think he had lovers. I wasn't so close to him, especially in later years. We disagreed about things.

Who was he?

She sighed and said, It's a long story, but you have access to Google no doubt.

I take this as a definitive dismissal of my line of questioning. I turn around and stand facing her.

Anna, it's so banal it almost makes me laugh. He died in the usual way, a heart attack. In the bathroom as it happens, and I discovered that he had a mistress and that flat I'm in downstairs was their love nest. I found her things everywhere. And his too. Even the bed.

I stop. I put my hand to my stomach, a reflex, but the pain doesn't come. That takes me by surprise and for a moment I smile. Then I say, So I'm running away, but I find myself running towards his secrets, his secret life. He died in debt, in terrible debt. In fact, maybe he died because of the debt because it was his heart that killed him. And I'm running away from his debt. As they say, I have repudiated it. Or I'm trying to. I'm entitled to shelter from the storm that he made, the ruins it left. Just because he was married to me doesn't mean I'm responsible for him. I wasn't his keeper. Was I? Yes I chose him, but I didn't choose his recklessness. I never even saw that side of him.

She lifts her glass to me but does not say a word. I walk to the table and pick mine up and clink it to hers.

We both drink, silently watching each other, I wondering what is going through her head. Perhaps the same thought occurs to her. And then she is telling me that she wants to go out to the balcony, she wants to see the moon and she doesn't trust herself outside at night when she is alone, what a gift it is that I am here. She offers me her arm and she leans on me as she rises. Unsteadily, arm in arm, we make our way out into the moonlight.

Something has gone wrong with the sea. I heard it as soon as I opened the shutters. And as I leave the house the grinding roar of sea on stone dominates the air. Without so much as a lift of wind, a breath of it, a huge storm has arisen. The flags along the front hang undisturbed while the sea mounts into enormous waves that course in upon the stony shore and fall like thunder. By the church the seas break almost as high as the belfry. There are several houses with windows that look out onto it and now they are shuttered and drenched with spray. I have no key to understanding this windless storm. It is counter-intuitive, illogical, unprecedented in my experience. The scaffolding we erect to understand nature simply crumbles in the face of the inexplicable. I feel lost, sick, undermined, invalidated.

Two young boys play games with the waves beside the church, rushing away when the wave breaks, rushing back as it withdraws. No heartache troubles them, no nausea in the face of the thingness of the inexplicable. Youth is full of faith. The trick is not to be caught, not to be drenched. We played it as children but with smaller waves. When they get caught they shout *Cazzo* and other casual obscenities. And a painter working on an easel stands well back and tries to capture in broad brush strokes the unaccountable ocean and the serenity of the sky.

Mare, Mer.

Muir in Irish. Sea comes from Anglo-Saxon, *sæ* in Beowulf. I also remember *wæg* for waves, *stream-as* for streams and *hwælweg* for whale way, the great Anglo-Saxon image called a *kenning*. There are whales here, I have learned, out there in the space between our mountain and Corsica is their *hwælweg.*

The heavy seas break white and globular, like exploding snow. Where do they come from? Corsica and Sardinia are a few hundred miles away at most. In Ireland the wave-trains start off Greenland or Newfoundland and have thousands of miles to build to their monstrous height. But this is a tiny sea parcelled up between Europe, Asia and Africa. And yet if these waves were falling on the stones of Aran they could not be worse. I am frightened by them. The noise and spume are overwhelming. I am standing in a fog and the sun is cold. The thunder and crash, the groaning of the hollow stones of the beach, the agony from the underworld, the ferocious suck and hiss as it withdraws. Whiteness everywhere, even the distant horizon speckled white and grey. And then the sea again. The noise, the noise. And again. And again.

Was I so steadfast all my days that nothing disturbed me? Even the land here is unsettled by the sea. *Il mare mangia la terra*, Anna said – the sea eats the land. I can see the bright polish of newly fallen stones under the cliffs of the Mountain of Portofino, mica scintillating in the winter sun. Teaching, living, travelling, *happy those early days when I shined in my angel infancy*. I had a husband, a house, a car, a job, friends both common and personal.

My life was a millpond, a mountain lake, going to work to teach, to meet, to talk, to write. The biggest question was who would be Head of School? Whose paper contradicted whose? But all the time his secret life was eating the ground from under me and I never noticed.

I have a sudden memory of a two-week sailing holiday he took. With whom did he go? Did he even go? He tried weakly to persuade me, knowing the very thought made me seasick. Whose boat was it? My brother-in-law Gerry's, maybe. They went down to the Isles of Scilly, then Brittany. He was to join them there, flying into Lorient. I left him at the airport drop zone. He hated goodbyes.

It seems to me that since I've been watching it the sea has settled slightly. The waves break less high. The noise is a few decibels lower.

I turn away to find the looming houses, the medieval archway, the ancient citadel, the tiny bars and restaurants palely gleaming golden in the sun, flat as cardboard cut-outs even though I know that the mass of their structures rising so many floors on the stony shore contains its own latent energy and that they radiate heat and light enough to warm a heart or a soul. Maybe even mine. My head is full of the rumour of change.

I have left my phone to discharge silently on airplane mode. But now I am thinking of changing to an Italian SIM, so I power it up again. I can't resist checking the messages. There are twenty-seven missed calls from a variety of numbers, some of which I don't recognise. There are five voice messages. I listen to them. The first is a sombre message from my ex-husband's solicitor saying that some of my husband's institutional creditors have combined and have informed him that they intend to go to court; unless I respond immediately I won't have a leg to stand on; if I engage with the creditors I have at least some chance of negotiating a reduced settlement but once the court is involved costs will escalate very quickly; he has seen how these companies work, so call back immediately. I replay the full message and count four uses of the word *immediately*.

For your information, Mick Cussen, there is no immediately here.

The next voice message is from my sister. She is furious. How dare you fucking walk out and dump this shit on me and Gerry, do you realise how many calls we've had from your fucking wanker of a solicitor— I delete it before it's finished. The next call is also from her; I delete it without listening. The third call is from an unknown number and consists only of someone breathing. It is not heavy breathing, but it is masculine; the word stertorous comes to mind. Someone whom I can imagine with a thatch of hair in his nose and a lugubrious expression. I am pleased that these half-forgotten words come so easily to mind. I listen for the full minute that it takes until the stertorous one hangs up, and then I delete that. I am about to delete the next call too, because it comes from my sister, but I play it by mistake and before I can correct my error I hear my sister say, Kate, call me, Gerry is in this too, and he's not the only one, he put money into something your stupid prick of a husband suggested, call me or I'll fucking slaughter you, call me now, we're getting calls ... just calls, so you better get back to me, fast. By the end of the message she is crying.

I sit down hard.

After a time I steady my breathing. I ring my sister. I hang up before the call connects. I repeat the performance. Each time I panic at the thought of what he did. How many others have been screwed by the bastard? The image comes to me of a disease spreading from cell to cell then from person to person. Some kind of rotting disease, a plague. A black death. I can smell my own sweat, my heart is thundering in my breast, I cannot think straight. Stop, I tell myself, do nothing. In this state I must do nothing. The temptation to do something stupid is almost too great. I get up slowly and go to the sink. I pour a glass of water and drink it in slow sips. I am outside my body watching myself holding the glass, tilting it to my lips, my throat working. Even from where I stand, at a distance, I can hear the hammering heart, smell the sweat. My hand is shaking. My head will not work properly, no thoughts are happening, at least not in the sense that I normally think of as thoughts, they have no organisation, just random words. What kind of calls is she getting? I'm trapped, people know, what did he do, he's dead and I can't ask, what am I doing? I don't know how long I remain at the sink, but I have a second glass of water. Then I pick up the keys and go out. I lock the door. I go upstairs. I knock on Anna's door. I can hear Michela hoovering elsewhere in the house. I knock again. Then I see that there is a bell button and I press it. The other evenings when I came for my lessons or for dinner this door was open and the lights from the dining room flooded the stairwell.

When the door opens she is in her dressing gown. She starts when she sees me. She says something in a mixture of Italian and French, two linguistic formulations for shock. Then she says, Come, sit, sit down.

She waves me in and I walk past her and sit on a chair near the window.

What has happened, Katy? You have seen a spectre?

I shake my head. I feel physically unable to speak. I look at her pleadingly and look away again. I become aware that my mouth is open and I close it. Then I open it again because it's harder to breathe. She goes out of the room. I am left alone sitting on this chair with the light from the sea slanting in on my left and rippling across the ceiling. I start to think about where she could have gone, why she left me in this state, and after a time I notice that my breathing has returned to something close to normal.

Then she returns carrying a glass of some clear liquid. She hands it to me.

I am sorry it was such a long time, but my back does not work and I had to get on my knees to find the bottle. It has been in the cabinet for a very long time. It's all I have. Drink it.

I swallow a gulp and my mouth, throat and chest turn to fire. I gasp. The shock is immense. I throw myself back in the chair and try to imagine what she could have given me. Sulphuric acid? Petrol? Cleaning fluid? Then the burning passes. I hand her the glass. It is still half full.

It is not good?

It's poison. What is it?

The grappa, a good one too.

She sits down in front of me and absentmindedly sips from my glass.

Now tell me what has happened.

I take a deep breath and explain about the voice message. I don't know what's happening, I say, but I know my husband has done something terrible.

I tell her about the minute-long silent call. As I tell her I realise that there is still one remaining unheard voice message. I take my phone out and look at it.

Play it, she says, let us hear the worst.

I don't recognise the number when the weird message-box voice tells me about it. The beginning of the recording is silent, maybe five seconds, but long enough for the pain in my stomach to return with a vengeance. I think I can detect the stertorous breathing. Then a deep female voice says, Mrs Holohan, I'm just leaving this message to say that your cleaning is ready and we're wondering if you forgot it because it's not like you to leave it so long at all at all, sorry for calling your mobile but the house wasn't answering, sorry, thanks very much, bye bye bye.

By the time she ends the message we are both laughing so hard that Anna has to put the glass down. I hold my sides and tears stream down my face. Anna keeps repeating the same phrase, *Che meraviglia! Che meraviglia!* When the laughter eases I reach across and take the glass and drink another gulp of fire and she gets up and goes to the other room and comes back with the bottle and a second glass.

Not all storms here are without wind. On a day of days, a sky torn by lightning, clouds boiling, shape-changing, monsters of darkness and fire, the air itself suffused with a mustard brown so that to look out was to see through a smoked glass, in the endless rolling and banging and shaking of thunder, a wind falls from the sky, twisting as it falls, gaining speed, turning and taking all before it; on the sea it is an intense bullseye of seething white water and steam; and it passes along the coast, ripping roof tiles, whole roofs, open windows torn like paper. I am working at my desk under the window, trying to read a newspaper I bought three days before. It is old news, but it is an exercise. I have Anna's dictionary open beside me. *Contestatore* was the last word I searched for. Protestor, demonstrator.

When I lift my eyes at the noise I am paralysed by shock. I can see the wind, a horn half-water half-air, a cornucopia of vapour or water, plastic bags, seaweed and a thousand nameless objects big and small. I watch it twist its way along the shore and then veer inland. Along the way it extracts trees from the soil and throws them away again, rolls boats on the hard-standing, capsizes potted plants and motorbikes. Café awnings evaporate. Restaurant chairs and tables, umbrella stands. Later I will read that it twisted through Recco paralysing the Savona train in the middle of the bridge and lifting one carriage off the track but not dropping it on the streets below where the population waited in frozen horror. It spins up the coast and heads for Ruta and the mountain, passing my house on the way. The noise alerts me to its coming, a roar like a train passing into a tunnel, tappings and hammerings and things falling out of the wind – stones, tools, broken glass – and then an ominous drumming. I feel the breath being sucked from me. The whole house sighs deeply. I can feel the drop in pressure in my ears like descending suddenly from a great height. I am too late or too frightened to secure the shutters and the wind flails them against the wall, smashing the frames and scattering the vanes. Then it is gone up the road to wreak its havoc on my neighbours' houses.

It takes three minutes all but a few seconds. From somewhere west of Recco to the mountain.

I stand at the window staring at the same blackening sky, the same clouds twisting and breathing like a damaged animal.

What about Anna?

I rush upstairs. I ring her bell and am alarmed when she doesn't come. Anna! I call, Anna!

After the freight train of the storm, the relative silence is frightening. What if another one comes? Perhaps it's the beginning of some terrible atmospheric calamity, like an earthquake in air. What if the storm plucked Anna from her balcony? I am about to hammer on the door with my fist when it opens and Anna stands there in her slip and bare feet.

What's happening, she says, why are you ringing my bell? I was asleep. It's the hour of the nap.

She is annoyed. After lunch she always says, *Schiacciamo un pisolino*. We'll take a nap. But the verb *schiacciare* means to crush or squash. One of those untranslatable constructions. Her nap usually lasts two hours and sometimes three. Nothing must disturb her. This is one of the many ironies of old age, she said once, that we sleep better in the day than the night.

Did you see the wind? I was worried about you!

Nobody can see the wind, Kate. Anyway, I was asleep. What has happened?

I tell her about my shutters, about the white water, the chimney of wind, noise. She stares at me and shakes her head. She thinks I'm mad. I take her out onto her balcony and show her, on either side, the three-minute path of destruction – roof tiles shattered, scattered on the ground, a Vespa on its side, sprawled across the road, scaffolding tilting dangerously away from a building on the other side, a tree down across a roof.

Madonna! she says, it's like the war.

Fausto wears battle fatigues and a white cotton cap. He brings his bag of tools. He speaks no English, but a crystal-clear Italian. I learn the word for shutter, vane, frame, joint, glue, break, piece. As well as other things – parachute, military, rifle, boar, hunt. It turns out that he was in the parachute regiment for national service, that he broke his leg on a jump, that he is a crack shot, that he is licensed to kill boar in the national park because there are too many of them, so many that they destroy people's gardens and have even come into the town to destroy the plants in Piazza Colombo, that he paints Anna's house every few years, that his daughter sometimes sells eggs when there are eggs. He has a heavy beard shadow and bright eyes. His voice is soft and somewhat musical, a lilt in it that places the first part of any phrase on a higher note than the rest. He has a tendency to repeat things in different pitches, which makes understanding easier.

The shutters, he shows me, have been shaken out of their frames and some of the vanes are broken but it would cost a thousand or more to have new ones made. Yes, more than a thousand certainly. He doesn't even know, it might be a lot more. He can glue them all together, perhaps a screw or two where necessary. Yes, a screw here and here perhaps. The best screws, the top, marine grade so they don't rust because the sea is not far away.

I have few words to talk with in this new world of wood and stone and steel, and so I listen, I nod, I say yes sometimes. It is an achievement even that I can hear the words as words. Not so long ago it was almost babble.

His patience reassures me. He is a gentle man.

He begins almost every sentence with *niente ma*..., nothing but ... It is a declaration of humility or self-abnegation.

He works patiently to collect the parts and places them in separate plastic boxes, which I realise are the kind that are used to store vegetables at the market. He puzzles over the vanes, which are all mixed up on the terrace, and sometimes offers them up to the frames to confirm his guess. He writes out an estimate in pencil and signs with a flourish. The pencil is IKEA, he says, he has hundreds of them, hundreds. And he gives me a present of two from the pocket of his khaki fatigues. I am grateful for the pencils and relieved that the estimate is not as bad as I expected. I am not in Ireland now, I tell myself.

He takes the jigsaw of the shutters away with him in his little three-wheeled lorry and in their absence I am disturbed by the brightness. I feel as if I am living inside a pale and translucent sea, or a glass case in an aquarium, and anyone passing can watch me. At night the blank darkness terrifies me and I keep the lights off as much as possible.

And he returns four days later and hangs the shutters in place and everything works. We contemplate them together and he smiles his radiant smile at my satisfaction. It is not so much a smile as a winter yielding to spring.

In a carefully rehearsed thank you, I tell him that he is like the magician in Philip Marlowe's play, also called *Fausto*. Philip Marlowe was an English writer. I do not say that Marlowe's Faustus conjures devils. He thanks me but says that he is named for a local saint, yes a saint; one of the stairways that goes up the mountain is called Salita San Fausto, he says. His wife jokes about it. She says he is no saint. The word for a joke is *scherzo*. I knew that even before I came to Italy. He demonstrates how to open and close the shutters carefully, and warns me to secure them as soon as I open them. He writes out the bill in IKEA pencil and signs it. He has given me a reduction, he says. The word for reduction is *sconto*. It appears to be one of that strange class of words where the meaning is changed by the addition of s at the start. I assume the root is *conto*, an account or bill. And I see he has taken ten per cent off. I pay him and he countersigns the bill and gives me the pencil as a present. Then very solemnly he shakes my hand and says he will call upstairs to Anna to salute her. Anna is an old friend, yes a very old friend.

I knock on her door even though it is open. Light streams through in flitters from the big balcony windows. It shimmers. The sea is in love with the sun, it never stops talking about it. The sun is relentless and unchanging, but the sea makes it dance and glitter. Most people here keep their shutters closed all day, but Anna needs light. She calls me in. And as I enter I meet a man coming out. He wears a fine tweed jacket with a coloured silk handkerchief in the breast pocket. His shoes are patent leather.

Hello, you are Anna's Irish friend?

Taken aback that he should address me in English, all I can do is agree.

He holds his hand out. Guido, he says.

Kate, I say.

He holds my hand for a second. If I can ever be of any help, Anna has my cell number.

Just then Anna emerges from her study, smiling. Guido, I think you should take Kate to San Fruttuoso, she has never been there. And you work too hard. Take a day off.

He looks at me dubiously.

It would give me pleasure, he says in Italian. If Kate would like to go.

What is San Fruttuoso? I ask, a little irritably. The import of my question is why would I bother to go. As far as I know it is a tourist trap out on the peninsula. I have watched the ferries laden with schoolkids and hikers setting out from the port.

Anna laughs. This is why we travel to places, to find out what they are.

I object that I can't really afford to waste money on frivolity. Again Anna's clear mischievous laugh. Don't worry, it is a twenty-minute boat ride. It's not Timbuktu.

I object that I am not good in boats and waves make me nervous, but somehow it is settled by the preceding exchange. I don't know at what point I agreed, or they assumed my agreement, a moment elided in an excess of goodwill. This man is taking me someplace. Anna assures me it is beautiful. He is less certain. I am the reluctant object of these contractual arrangements. What is more, I smell a rat. Anna is matchmaking and I have no desire to match or be matched. One man was enough for me. I wonder if there is an Italian proverb to compare with once bitten twice shy.

Anna is peeling a blood orange, the flesh so bloody it is black as clotted arterial blood. The rush of illicit sweetness from the dark flesh. By now I know it well.

Then his courteous nod of the head, something quizzical in his look, his *alla prossima* as though a next time is a certainty, and he walks past me. I hear him going down the stairs, his leather-soled shoes battering the steps. He was, I realise, almost as uncomfortable as me about the set-up.

Today there was mimosa for sale for the Day of the Women. The young Arab boy selling it, his sweet wounded eyes. He was perhaps fifteen. He spoke French. He came from Morocco, he said, through Catania, there were hundreds on his boat. I have brought a sprig for Anna. She hugs me and thanks me, telling me that the tradition began at the end of the war when the homecoming mountain partisans brought the flower to the women. She goes off to find a vase, and I am left with the feeling of having held something mechanical in my arms, like a small engine or the parts of an engine, full of the energy of its own breaking.

On my way here, on the steps of Salita del Priaro a lemon fell at my feet – the tree, in someone's garden, laden with yellow lights. I put the fruit in my pocket, feeling guilty as though such a theft made anyone poorer or me richer, and I thought of Anna and of the bounty she had brought to my days.

It's obvious you need a job, Anna Ferrara said. She meant something to occupy my time, but also because soon the money will run out if I continue drawing on savings.

I propose to you teaching, she said.

Then she took an address book from a drawer and studied it for a few moments. I guessed she was looking for contacts. At one point she said, What a pity, he would be perfect but he's dead. She opens the drawer again and takes out a pen and crosses his name off. He was younger than me, she said, and one of those arrogant men who thought I as a woman enjoyed having my ass touched in the *ascensore*, the lift you say? Or the elevator? Imagine what I did? He was behind me. He was already a big one in the party and he played the big-I-am. Do you say that? We say, *Se la tira*. It means more or less the same but is perhaps a little more rude. I won't explain the etymology if you don't mind.

But what did you do, I said, amused by her digression.

Oh he stroked my ass and I turned around and slapped his face. Then the lift doors opened and some other women came in and that was the end of that. Strange, but he was never angry about it afterwards. We were almost friends. He would have loved to patronise a beautiful young foreign woman like you and you could have used that to get a small teaching job at the university. He was a powerful man. But he's dead. And I'm still alive. *C'est la vie*, no? And as that idiot Benigni said in his ridiculous film about Auschwitz, *la vita è bella*.

She stared at me smiling and I marvelled for the first time that she needed no glasses for reading or distance. Her eyes were a soft brown, almost hazel colour. They were beautiful.

It was a ridiculous film, she said, because it has no politics. Without politics we cannot understand fascism. Sympathy is a variable. I was never a feminist because it seemed to me that equality was obvious, one could not be a communist and not be feminist so I was a communist first and a woman second. But there were plenty of men who thought equality was something for men, communists too, not just the fascists. Now I'm not so sure that I should have stayed outside the struggle. Women are the first to be poor, the first to go hungry, the first to lose their jobs.

She wrote out a name and a number. This is a young man, well he was a young man twenty years ago when I knew him. I know he is still alive because he writes things. He loves Yeats, too. You should call him and explain that you need work, part-time you say? and ask if there are classes. They are always looking for someone.

And so I am sitting in the wintry sun outside a café in a square in Genoa. A genial browned-skinned man is working his way along the single line of outside tables offering Kashmir shawls and scarves for sale. Most people ignore him. One girl feels the material and chats to him but rejects it in the end. When he comes to me he speaks English without prompting. I wonder how he knows. I've noticed the beggars have the same skill. Is it an aura? Or the way I dress? Or the colour of my skin? I have been thinking about Joyce again. I miss teaching. This morning I woke with the memory of Dedalus's exchange with Mr Deasy about debt. What is the Englishman's proudest boast? Mr Deasy thinks it is that he paid his way, never borrowed a shilling. He asks Stephen if he can feel that satisfaction and Stephen silently enumerates his own debts: *Mulligan, nine pounds, three pairs of socks, one pair brogues, ties. Curran, ten guineas. McCann, one guinea,* and so on. Joyce himself was an expert on debt having spent most of his life in it. The memory warms me to a smile. I have no debts, I tell myself. My husband's I renounce. Why should the law of heredity apply to one who renounces the heritage? It is like the Catholic Church telling an atheist that he can never escape being a Catholic.

As it happens I am sorry that I agreed to sit outside. A sharp northerly breeze is blowing from the snow-topped Apennines behind the littoral. It chills the coast, and Genoa, Anna told me, is always cold. So when he comes to my table I ask about a rich black and red shawl. When he says seventy I laugh and he laughs too, a huge smile that warms me. I make hard bargain, he says. He says fifty. Eventually I buy it for twenty-five. Along the way I discover that he is from Bangladesh and that he has just come back from holidays there, where he saw his wife and children. I feel guilty and give him thirty and when he insists on giving back the five I try to refuse it but fail. Surprisingly he offers his hand and when I take it I am struck by its gentleness and softness. I wonder what he did for a living in Bangladesh. He waves as he crosses the street heading for a group of tourists having the equestrian statue of Garibaldi explained to them. At least Garibaldi said he was a socialist even if he didn't know what it meant, I think, remembering what Anna said.

Then a tall, thin, elegantly dressed man of about sixty is speaking to me. It takes a few seconds to realise he is mispronouncing my name. *Signora Oloan?* I shake hands and invite him to sit.

A waitress is there immediately and he orders a coffee for himself and a cappuccino for me. His Italian is so clear it is almost translucent. Again I feel pleased with myself for recognising words and phrases. I can understand some of them or guess at them. His poise takes my breath away. Every word, every movement, every gesture is economical and exact and, at the same time, as elegant as a dancer's.

I catch myself checking his ring finger and finding it without a ring or even the trace of a ring.

Che peccato, he is saying, what a pity, there is not a place in the department at the moment, but there are some students that he knows who would happily pay for private lessons. He could think of two names immediately. If I wanted to write out my email or telephone number he could pass them on to anyone interested, he says, handing me his pen. He watches as I write them out. I am conscious of his gaze. He is studying my face. A sudden crazy looseness enters me, a wash of pleasure and wantonness that I have not felt in many a year. I try to remember the last time I had sex. It takes me back years, the sameness of nights when he was out at meetings, away on business, tired, when I got used to his indifference, when I began to feel that I had aged badly and that my body was no longer desirable, when in fact I repressed, submerged, drowned at birth my own desires. When I stopped desiring him. I look sideways at this stranger and smile and he smiles too, and we hold each other's gaze for whatever that time is that psychologists have identified as significant and expressive of desire. Then I hand him my telephone number and my email and he takes a wallet from his inside jacket pocket and folds the note into it. I put the top back on the pen and give it back. He smiles and I smile.

I'm afraid I must take my leave, he says with a look of almost comical sadness. He stands and I stand too. Also you leave?

I nod and he takes my new Kashmir shawl and drapes it over my shoulders. His hands linger a little and then he squeezes each shoulder, leans in to kiss me on both cheeks, leans back to look at me with that sorry-to-leave-because-I-know-you'll-miss-me smile and walks away.

Now that he's gone and the sticky slick of desire has dispersed a little, I think: what a fucking slimy shit.

I shiver with revulsion. All that melting and smiling and seductiveness. I think: I was practically simpering. And then I realise he left the bill on the table. I put four euro coins on it and draw the waiter's attention. On the side of the pillar facing the street someone has sprayed the words *Fuck Austerity*, beside it a ring with an *A* inscribed in red. The words are in English. Underneath, like a punctuation mark, a five-pointed star with an arrow through it like a lovelorn heart. I walk into the cold wearing my Kashmir shawl like a breastplate. I could drive the elegant men and policemen from the square with my trusty sword, if I had a sword, and defend the young Japanese women and the beggars and the shawl-sellers against all comers. Come one, come all, I think.

I use washing-up liquid. I soap the finger well and work the ring against the joint. *Treasury bonds, maturing bills of exchange, IOUs, wedding rings, watchchains, lockets.* I have been working for ten minutes now without success. The joint is aching and feels bruised. Yesterday, when I was writing my email address and I knew he was watching, I saw my wedding ring as if for the first time. The thought occurred to me then: I'm still married to the fucker, dead and all as he is. Then: I'll fix that. Last night when I got home I tried for an hour. The flesh around my metacarpal was swollen, almost purple. This morning it has shrunk a little and I am determined. I go to the freezer and take out the ice-cube mould. I make up a glass of iced water. I push the ring back to the knuckle and put the joint into the cold water. The cold is intense. After a few minutes I add more ice cubes. It is almost painful. After a time, during which the ice cubes melt slowly, I soap the joint and push the ring. To my surprise it comes off without too much trouble. I laugh and place the ring on the sink. I remember seeing a Compro Oro shop somewhere. My finger feels light. There is, of course, the faded band of smooth skin; it will be there for a long time. I open the kitchen press and find a smoky shot-glass and drop the ring into it and place the glass in the far corner of the highest shelf. Hiding treasure.

I take a roll of bin bags from a drawer and go into the bedroom. I start to pile his clothes into the bags – jackets, jeans, shorts, shirts, socks, underpants. I swear as I work, fuck fuck fucker fucking bastard fucker. These resurgences of foul anger surprise me always. Until his death I rarely if ever uttered a profanity. But I also realise I am enjoying it. I'm dumping you, you fucker, into the bin, I hope they fucking recycle you, I hope you end up on someone who really needs clothes, a homeless person, because you always hated homeless people and beggars, or anyone who will value the fact that you bought fucking Armani jeans.

At home in Ireland, during the interregnum between his death and my flight, before I ran away, they happened more often, the swearing times. I wonder should there be mourning? Should there be grief? There are stages of mourning, I forget how many. What is my ordinal? The second stage? The third? When the bags are full I look with satisfaction at the space I have freed. I have begun to enjoy wearing her clothes and have studied the labels. Soon I will make a trip to Genoa to visit the shops. I now hope that my own suitcase never turns up – my last contact with the call centre in charge of it suggested that they had no idea what had become of it. I feel younger, but more importantly, it feels transgressive. I recognised that early on. I am wearing my husband's mistress's knickers. It has conferred a quasi-sexual power on me. Inside someone else's skin I feel the call of private places. I have been dreaming about sex, about luxurious rooms with painted ceilings and rococo furniture, about heat and sweat. But also about empty streets and shuttered shops and houses and rats. There is no bed of roses.

I feel intensely lonely at times, and filled with resentment that I can't stop missing him even though I hate him. And then I wonder whether I hate him most for dying or for fucking the little bitch. Anna Ferrara has given me a word she says she learned when she was working as a union organiser in factories around Naples. The word is *zoccola*. I am certain from the ceremony with which she produced it that I will never be in a position to use it in speech in the presence of Italians. It has the ring of the forbidden. Anna said it was hateful, which is exactly what I need. I google it and discover that it stands for prostitute or sewer rat. The definition provokes a shiver of disgust at a language that can catalogue so precisely the position in the class hierarchy of a woman who is simply making a living in bad circumstances. Specifically a sewer rat, not a house rat or a field rat or a rat in general. I wonder if there is a male equivalent but the Garzanti online dictionary tells me that *zoccolo* (with the masculine ending) means a clog, a hoof, a clod, a plinth, a skirting board, a shoe, a valve base, or, oddly, but perhaps by metaphor, the hard core of a theory or argument. There are no rats in male prostitution.

And so, more than a little unwillingly, I begin to think of her as the *zoccola*.

In the *zoccola*'s panties.

Today's Italian lesson is to take place outdoors because, according to Anna, spring is here. I help her to the chariot of fire and unplug it from the wall. And she moves out into the road without looking behind her. She goes by the road and I take the shortcut over the railway bridge and down the steps that are not dark at this hour of the morning and this month of spring with the sun only just above the mountain. At the foot of the stairs I am greeted by Leo, standing outside his wine shop. Now I too buy my wine there. Yesterday he delivered six bottles of Barbera, the cheapest thing in the shop at four euro a bottle. I turn left and go down the steps beside the fisherman's co-operative and the bakery and then through the medieval arch. The café by the pier, at the back of the church, on the sunny side because the other side of the café looks out on the port and is good in the evening when people come out to stroll. *La Cage aux Folles*. Now I know the owner's name is Enrico. He is a handsome man with bright eyes and a ready smile. He calls me Kate but he calls her Signora Anna.

Will Signora Anna be here today?

He says it in English but I answer tentatively in Italian that yes, she will come. And he says *Brava*! I feel pleased. It was the future tense, even though for Italians the present also expresses the future, or that part of it that is proximate and a little uncertain. Behind him a bright, white seagull with an orange-yellow beak watches me out of one eye, standing on one foot on the seawall. I have lost pounds, kilograms, I don't know how much but the *zoccola*'s denims are no longer tight. I sometimes wonder what her hips looked like, what her bum looked like. I remember none of that, only her face.

And then Anna arrives. Enrico pulls a seat aside and gives her his hand. I am struck as always by how she manages to look both elegant and arthritic. She thanks him in French and he replies in French, bowing deeply as he does so, a little comedy of politesse.

Today, she says, we study the imperative. The imperative has only one tense: the present. It is used to issue a direct order, also to give instructions, express necessity, to exhort, advise and encourage – but it is always the present.

Anna is a hard taskmaster. When I accepted her offer of lessons I assumed they would be relaxed, would involve much digression and many of her usual observations about everything. In fact she is a ferocious disciplinarian. Once, when I joked about it, she said, rather mysteriously: I learned discipline when it was dangerous.

I take out my notebook and pen and she begins to describe the imperative mood.

A young woman stops by our table to speak to Anna and as she talks she stretches, sways, twists, inflates her chest, crosses and uncrosses her legs, smiles, simpers, pouts, lays a hand flat against her left breast, touches

Anna's cheek. In a conversation of three minutes duration she moves through every posture and gesture available to a human. A yoga of the affections. I wonder if she is in love with Anna. Then her little daughter, who has been chasing pigeons, calls and they leave together.

Coffee comes and Enrico looks over my notes and makes an approving sound. The church bells ring the hour of eleven. There are people sitting on the low stone seat that runs around the curved back of the church buildings. The ferry to San Fruttuoso is making its way over a gilded morning sea. A man is setting a net between here and Punta Chiappa and Radio Swiss Jazz is playing quietly through the speakers overhead. The incongruous imperative in this idyll. It cannot last. I imagine debt as something inexorable, all-consuming, a kind of cancer that lies hidden in the dark while it eats me from the inside. Suddenly, as I am writing the imperative of the irregular verb *andare*, to go (*vai, vada, andiamo, andate, vadano*), she puts her index finger on my ring finger, or my ex-ring finger, my left hand resting on the table beside my notebook, and when I look up she holds my gaze a moment before smiling and then that word again, softly spoken this time: *Brava*.

There is a bench a little below the level of my road. It is perfectly sheltered. There is a tall house on either side; the hill is at its back, and it faces south and west, a sunset always in its future. Ten shallow and irregular steps lead down to it and afterwards the path goes in two directions. One leads down to a little children's playground, the other leads more directly to the port. I bring Anna here when she is able. There are times when, from this lofty perch above the Mediterranean, the day seems bleached out, as though what I'm seeing is not colour but light itself. And evenings when the sun sinks leaving a bank of cloud in air-force blue, straight as a pencil line at the bottom and fretted with electric red from the sunset at the top. Such times I recall Pound, *But here in Tigullio / emerald over sapphire/ april birds thru the stillness*. He was down the road in Rapallo where the sea is called the Tigullio. And, as Anna often reminds me, he was a fascist not by accident or perforce but by intellect and desire. Still he caught and held the character of the light here, framed it in words. That is something surely.

I sit there in gentle silence watching the fishermen shooting nets, the container ships moving like lizards against the horizon, the ferry coming home from Corsica. In the evenings a street lamp illuminates it. Inside the globe a gecko lives, pleased to have found a warm place that attracts flies. He throws a shadow on the gable wall to the east magnified by distance. It is as if a dinosaur were moving silently between the houses.

I have brought you a book, Anna says, one evening when she had accompanied me to this haven. You must begin to read.

She hands me a tiny book called *Come Va Il Tuo Cervellino*. She explains that the phrase means How goes your little brain. It is an affectionate expression such as one might say to a child.

I laugh and tell her that the book is well suited to how I feel. Since he died I don't think I have had a coherent thought.

In any case, this is your first task, she says, opening the book at page fourteen. It is a little love letter. It is time that you began to think about love again.

Who is this Giulia Schucht that it's addressed to?

She was a musician, a violinist.

I notice that the letter begins, *Mia Carissima.*

Italian is such a beautiful language, I say, I know of no language that expresses affection so well.

Also it expresses the opposite very well, Anna Ferrara says. Then suddenly she begins to list the words that she says I must never say: *gnocca, figa, cazzo, porco dio.* Her breathless hush, her giggling like a girl, pinching my arm. By the end there are tears streaming down her face. *O Dio*, she says, it is so good to say what cannot be said! But you know, you cannot understand a language until you can swear in it. This is why pillow talk is so important. In French my favourite is *connasse!*

Passing on the road below, on the other side of the park, the old sailor who sat with me that night. He wears his sailor's cap at a jaunty angle this evening. He has his best suit on.

Who is that man?

Paolo is his name. He was a *primo macchinista* on the ships. How do you say it, first engineer?

Chief engineer.

Yes. He was the chief. His lungs are diseased. It is *asbestosi*. All the ships had *amianto*. You say asbestos? You can imagine. It was actually worse in the engine room of course. He told me once that all his *macchinista* friends have it. There is a state pension. It takes forty years after the exposure to become a disease. People say it is a good trick to pretend to have it but doctors are not so easily fooled. People always think the worst of their fellow man.

The thought reminds me of my father whose opinion of his fellow man never wavered. In memory, as so often in life, he is standing at the kitchen sink, his arms folded. My mother was long gone by then. How old was I? Fifteen perhaps. He is talking about miniskirts. That young one of the Healy's, he says, is asking for trouble, mark my words she'll be in the family way before the year is out, did you see the length of her skirt. And someone is agreeing. Who is it? Memory picks my father out like a single tree in a shaft of evening sunlight, but the landscape itself is blind to me. It could be my sister. It could be a neighbour. But one thing I know for certain is that the remark is about me. Because I tucked my school pinafore up to shorten it and I forgot to let it down again before getting off the bus and he happened to see me. That was his way. Everything was indirect, a cynical complainer about human nature who never believed in a cause or trusted another man or woman. When I read *Hamlet* in later years I recognised him as Polonius, the bumbling busybody setting spies, laying out money for information about his own son, the ineffectual old man who understood nothing of women. And still neither I nor my sister was Ophelia. We escaped that much at least. But when I went to my first dance he already knew who I had danced with by the time I woke up next morning. He had nothing but contempt for them, the disdain of a man who had taught most of the village and found them wanting. And he took pride in his informants. I know everything, missy, remember that. *And thus do we of wisdom and of reach, / With windlasses and with assays of bias / By indirections find directions out.*

The sun slants through everything like a dagger. We are looking out, from the relative discomfort of her old Beetle, on the long beach of Sestri Levante with its comfortable and elegant hotels and its beach establishments selling food and chairs. And though there are no chairs at this time of the year I can imagine them peopled with beautiful bodies, eating, talking, calling to children. I recall that scene from Jean Vigo's film *À Propos de Nice* in which a middle-class white man acquiring a tan on a deckchair on the beach is suddenly, and only for an instant, turned into the black man that he would despise but whose skin he longs for.

Anna resettles the rug over her legs. She seems distracted.

I want to walk the sand in the Baia del Silenzio, she says. It's just over there.

She sighs a little petulantly and I realise she means it.

And so I help her from the car. The verb is *scendere*, to descend, she tells me again. One descends from a car because one descended from a carriage. Language conserves history.

I take her arm and walk her past the church and through the town and down a narrow side street that leads to the sea. But it is the most perfect little place. The houses all turning their backs, right down onto the sand, and the convent on the southern side, and the boats.

We sit at a café that is right on the beach. There is sand at our feet. She spends a long time gazing at the sprinkling of yachts on swinging moorings. Some fishing boats hauled up on the sand, dismasted sailing dinghies. She is preoccupied and, I suspect, sad. After the waiter takes our order she says, I brought a dear friend here once, I have so many memories, sometimes I think old age is a dream and the memories are what is real.

I wish I could smoke, she says, I used to smoke, it was de rigueur for young ladies of my youth. Some time, I was maybe thirty, I decided I should give it up. I don't remember why. At my age I'm too old to be killed by it. Maybe I should begin again. But if I had continued I would be dead now and no longer possessed of the desire to smoke.

Then suddenly a dreamy look passes over her face. Look, she say softly, that woman in the green dress.

Her hand goes to her throat as though helping her to catch her breath and finds her gold chain. She closes her fingers over the locket. She does not point but there is no need to. Coming towards the café, her feet in the cold water, a pair of shoes in her hand, is a striking young woman, her hair cut tight and rough. Her dress is emerald green, long almost to her ankle and pleated from the waist, one hand bunching it out of the water. She is absorbed in watching the coming and going of the waves over her feet.

At the next table a baby is preparing to explode in tears. Ramping up half sobs, half wails, ignoring his mother's attempts to distract. A waiter comes and shakes some keys in front of him to no avail. Then he makes a face and the baby stops for three seconds before launching into a desolate wail. The mother gathers him up and the father pays the bill. All this time Anna is staring at the beach.

I want to go, she says. Please pay.

But you haven't finished your wine.

Vai, she says, hurry. I want to go home. At my age wine in the afternoon is bad for digestion.

I signal for the bill, but Anna is rising like a damaged machine, shifting weight onto her knees, leaning on the table, straightening insofar as she can straighten, shuffling to turn away and launching herself at a pace between the tables, bracing herself on occasional chair backs, headed for the exit and the sandy pathway home. The waiter comes with the bill and I pay him. I look again and the girl in the emerald dress is gone. Did we imagine her?

It was market day on Via della Repubblica. I went to the bank machine to draw five hundred from my own card. The secret card account was almost empty. My calculation was that there should be three thousand or so left in my own account in Ireland. But when I entered my PIN the screen message was: *Transaction refused*. My card reappeared. I went through the same process again but didn't dare try a third in case the card was swallowed by the institution. I felt the back of my head grow cold. My neck, then my face. They are closing me down, I thought, whoever they are. I stared for so long at the stupid faded screen that the person behind me tapped politely on my shoulder.

So I went to the supermarket and tried to buy a packet of coffee on my card and again the transaction was refused. The shame, the humiliation, the abject need to cry, to shout, to stamp my feet at people who would not understand a word but who would be entirely sympathetic if they could understand. I reminded myself that these things happen and that the supermarket customers do not know I am an absconding debtor, but the rising tide of shame cannot be diverted.

I paid in cash. I left without making a scene. I walked down Via della Repubblica and through the arches and up Salita del Priaro and through my gate and into the house and up the stairs to Anna Ferrara's apartment still carrying my packet of Pellini Top like an unexploded bomb. When she opened the door I presented it to her in a daze, and she invited me in. Already at nine o'clock in the morning she was fully dressed in a tweed skirt, silk blouse and cardigan, but she was wearing her sheepskin slippers with little bobbles of sheep on them. She invited me into her study, which was in fact, a second bedroom and which looked out on the same view as my sitting room but from an elevated position. There were books piled on her desk and a mass of neatly typed paper. The typewriter was an Olivetti.

She sat at the neat office chair in front of her desk and I sat on the old straw-seated chair beside it. Tell me, she said. And so I told her that at long last my accounts have been blocked. I have no further access to my savings at home.

What is more, they will have a record of where the transactions had been happening. They'll know where I am.

The wailing and clacking of seagulls on rooftops. Sometimes they sound like angry cats. The sound of boat engines. The sound of helicopter engines. Contrails like a basketwork to hold the sky up.

I told her that I was beginning to think they wouldn't come for my accounts, that they would content themselves with everything else, all of the accoutrements of a well-lived life disappearing into the maw of unconscionable debt, my house, my furniture, my clothes, my car, even my friends. My sister too, because Gerry for all his training in money couldn't sniff out a rogue investment when it was presented to him. All that ridiculous world of percentages and dividends and contracts. All spivs, all sharks dressed as mannequins talking their big-man talk about playing hard ball and fucking people over and what is my handicap and which school did I go to, and their whole raison d'être is making money and when it comes down to it, the only way they can do it is by cheating and even then they make a mess of that and have to be saved from bankruptcy by people who haven't two brown pennies to rub together. They're dependent on the poorest of the poor to save them by giving up even more of their lives to filling out forms.

Who are you talking about, Anna Ferrara says. Not your husband.

I stop suddenly and think.

Yes, I say, he's part of that world. I know I was talking about the crash, but he's just another shark in a suit. He was. I mean the economic crash in Ireland.

You're talking about class, she said, and money. Let me tell you about money.

She pauses for a moment. I recognise the expression on her face by now. She is collecting her thoughts.

He who can buy bravery is brave, she says, though he be a coward. As money is not exchanged for any one specific quality, for any one specific thing, or for any particular human essential power, but for the entire objective world of man and nature, from the standpoint of its possessor it therefore serves to exchange every quality for every other.

Something tells me it is a text she learned a long time ago. I can almost see her searching in her head for the words. In what context did she learn them? Or is she translating from Italian as she goes? And where does the text come from? It has a beauty to it, a poetry, for all its hard-headedness. It is less an advice and more a recitation.

But my head is full of the fog of transience, of the dream invoked by her declaration that she wanted to tell me about money, the great incubus of debt lurking in the shadows at the edge. A waking will come. At this moment I cannot imagine still being here in a week. How do they find debtors? An absconded debtor. A defaulter. I have read of cases where people were pursued through the courts. Even to America. But they were very big fish, corrupt bankers and venture capitalists. Not people who lecture in modernism.

And she is holding my hand and I am watching the blood pulsing in her veins and I think, I love this woman, she is ninety years of age and here she is quoting poetry to me in English to console me for being bankrupt. Who says poetry makes nothing happen?

Now she opens a drawer in her desk and takes out a chequebook in a little leather case. She flips it open and says, How much do you need? I have no children.

We neither of us, I think; no children, no future. I hear Macduff in his terrible realisation that there can be no revenge: *He has no children. All my pretty ones.*

I shake my head. No, I say, no thank you. I don't need money yet. I'm going to contact that man I met in Genoa and take some pupils. I don't need much to live here.

Brava, she says, *no pasaran!*

But, she says, you told me he was a shit. I think you said shit.

I laugh. Yes, I did say shit.

Money, she says, is nothing and everything, but most of all it is a figment of the imagination. We need it to live among our neighbours, to buy food, but if it vanished into the air like a bubble we would simply find another way. There are other ways to live. And it does vanish like a bubble. Look at how, when they needed to, the great central banks just printed more. Why couldn't they print more to buy houses for the poor? For the people whose jobs vanished because of so-called restructuring? That's what happened to you. You had money and then, you had nothing, less than nothing for even your future was owed to someone else. But you have your labour and your skill, and labour and skill are the links of the golden chain we have forged for ourselves.

So instead she picks up the telephone and enters a number. She waits for a moment. When the person at the other side answers I hear her say, *Buonasera cara compagna*. Good evening dear companion. After that I am lost in the speed of the conversation. I wonder idly why she calls the person at the other end her dear companion. I noted the feminine forms of *cara* and *compagna*. I can't hear the voice. I pick up chance phrases including the ever-present *Irlandese*, but also now, *cerca lavoro*, meaning she is looking for work, and that polychromatic Italian concept, *simpatica*. I wonder if, in this world of brilliant women, I should only learn feminine endings. In the end she is nodding and saying, Yes, yes, of course. She says goodbye, *grazie carissima*, and hangs up.

She grimaces and says, She is one of those people who says *ciao* ten times before she hangs up.

She takes a sheet of notepaper and writes out a name, address and phone number.

I make a rough translation in my notebook. The uneven progress of my Italian. There are days when I distinguish almost every word heard, and days when the fog drifts in from the cold seas of memory and I can only think in English, sometimes even in Irish or French, one language substituting smoothly for the other, spies slipping across linguistic borders, putting on uniforms, making a fool of me. Hybrid sentences, tenses, cases, moods.

Today even a rough version takes forever. *My dearest, how have you saved me from becoming a complete stick-in-the-mud. The instinct for rebellion which.* Italian seems to use too few commas and too many. Too few full stops perhaps. *The instinct for rebellion which from childhood was against the rich, the reason why I couldn't go on with my studies, I who got ten in everything in elementary school, while the children of the butcher, of the pharmacist and of the fabric salesman went to secondary school.* What kind of a love letter is this? Who is this man complaining about his education? How often does someone get ten in everything in primary and then fail at secondary? The man is a whinger, I think, as the sun sets in my window and I have to think about food. But I press on, the habits of the scholarly life telling me that at least a first draft is needed before eating. *I enlarged this [resentment?] to the rich who oppressed the poor farmers of Sardinia and who I thought should fight for national independence for the island. Into the sea with the continentals: how many times did I repeat this slogan.* I never knew that there was a Sardinian independence movement. How little I know about this country. *Then I came to know the working class of an industrial city and I understood the meaning of the stuff from Marx that I first read out of intellectual curiosity. Thus I became impassioned for life, for the struggle, for the working class. I kiss your eyes, my dear, for a long long time, to give you strength, to scatter all the dark clouds, because you are strong strong, as you can be, as you must be, my companion.* Or perhaps *My comrade.*

Comrade. When she says *cara compagna* she means dear comrade. Not dear companion.

What a strange love letter.

When I talk to Anna about it she has to touch her eyes with her sleeve and then blow her nose on a cotton handkerchief. Old age is full of ambushes, she says.

There is that burned coffee smell that comes from the Bialetti on the gas. And already she has the tray with the little coffee cups and the bowl of sugar in cubes. It is the only sweet thing she likes. Sometimes she spoons it out when the coffee is finished. The sugar in the bottom of the coffee cup is the poor man's dessert, she says. She is sitting by the balcony window with the sun at her back. She wears a pleated plaid skirt and silk blouse with a silk bow to tie the neck. Her shoes are Oxford brogues polished to a mirror. Her uniform.

Today there will be no lesson, She says. I am tired. Guido and I had a long chat on the telephone. He asked if you were well. Of course I told him you are a hero. Guido is a good man, a kind man. He too has had his troubles. He lost his wife some years ago. They had no children. Of course I have no personal experience, but I think children can be a consolation at such times. I have observed it. Come sit with me and I will tell you the names for the dangerous liaisons of old age. You will recognise many. *Artrite, artritico.*

Arthritis, arthritic? Is Guido your doctor?

She laughs. No, no, I worked with his father. I've known Guido since he was a child.

She waves her hand dismissively. As if I would confide my ailments to a handsome young man! At my age all doctors should be fat and bald. *Bronchite?*

Bronchitis?

Esatto. You see? It's easy. *Vene varicose, pressione sanguigna, insonnia, stitichezza, psoriasi.* I take pills and then I take pills for the pills. Pills to fix something and the pill to fix the thing caused by the pills to fix it. I sometimes think I should set up a little private pharmacy. Are you familiar with the concept of an infinite regression? I could cure any ailment. Growing old is not worth the effort, but not growing old is not something to celebrate either. Of the two, I prefer the first. Disease is a good word in English, she says. It is indeed dis-ease. She laughs and the laugh is infectious.

In any case, the verb for suffer is *soffrire.* Conjugate it for me. She has a way of waving her hand that suggests a command.

Dutifully I work through the past, present, future and conditional of the verb to suffer.

Brava, she says.

Then, softly, in Italian, she says, We two have suffered.

And equally quietly I say, Yes.

The minor corrections. *Soffriremo*, we will suffer. *Soffrirei*, I would suffer.

Anna, I say, I feel so inadequate when I speak to you.

I have to explain inadequate as it's not a usage she has encountered before.

I grew up in a little village in rural Ireland. My father was a kind man even though he was severe with us girls. I don't think he understood women. I suppose losing my mother made him uncertain. Just because he couldn't love my mother or she couldn't love him didn't mean that he wasn't a good person. I had a happy childhood as these things go.

Her gaze is intense.

The poet Spaziani says: We are all children of peasants, in every attic there are suitcases tied with cord, yet we are doctors, we hang our diplomas on the walls.

Thank you, I say.

I too, she says, had a happy childhood. I loved my father and my mother. I had two sisters and I loved them too. But my father was one of those who volunteered to fight for Franco. He was an airman. He went to Spain. He thought fascism was the future.

And you still loved him?

Why not? He was my father.

But he was still a fascist.

Yes and it wasn't until we declared war on the English, which we did for Hitler, that he realised he was wrong and by then it was too late. He loved England. He thought Hitler was a maniac and Mussolini should never have made friends with him. He thought Italian fascism was different.

And was it?

No.

She leans back, eyes closed. Her face drawn and grey.

He tried to stop me, she says, when he realised my politics. He even tried to stop me going to university but my mother rebelled. Men were powerful in those days and a girl should marry and have children. It was always a struggle. In the party too, it was all men at the top. But when my father was dying he told me that he regretted everything. He said fascism wasted his life. And not only his life but the lives of millions. The worst thing was the Jews, he said, but everything else was almost as bad.

I had good relations with my male colleagues, Anna. I never had to fight the patriarchy as you did.

But, she says, in the end ...

Yes, I say, in the end a man screwed it up.

She laughs.

I like how you face up to things, Katia.

She has taken to calling me Katia and sometimes even Katyusha. Once she even hummed an air I recognised as Russian. We sing that here too, she said, but it is not a love song.

My sister says I don't face up to it, that I ran away.

Why should you be responsible for your husband's debts? You didn't contract them. What is the word to cause a debt, I know it, but it doesn't come into my mind?

To incur?

Yes, to incur. In Italian I can use the same word, *incorrere*. But we tend to say contract, *contrarre*. But you did not personally incur these debts. They are yours by law of inheritance. Law is just a mystification of the power of the rich. It's an ideological form like the others. Inheritance is among the worst of these laws.

But law is what we have.

She makes a dismissive gesture. Drink your coffee before it grows cold.

Once, I say, my father tried to sell a piece of land that he bought with a view to putting a holiday caravan on it. He was advised to first of all secure planning permission

116

so that the person buying it knew they could build on it. But when he applied for permission the neighbour whose garden bordered it put up all sorts of objections and permission was refused. My father was very angry. He set the piece of land aside and never touched it again. It went to weed and brier. It became a wilderness right beside the garden of the man who objected to planning permission. It was my father's revenge. But his dying wish was that the land should be cleared and re-sown with grass. He wanted to make amends. Except that the man he wanted to make amends to was already dead, it's just my father didn't know it. We never told him.

She nods.

In those days, I say, we had very few photographs. Of my mother, I had four. Only in one of them was she alone. In that photograph she is looking down, she has a hat on her head which gives it a little shade. She looks happy and tranquil. But I have wished all my life for her to lift her eyes in the photograph and look at me. Just one time. To know that I am here.

I realise I have told the story in Italian. I realise, in retrospect, that there were many errors, that in English I would have been more precise, but somehow the story has been told despite my incompetence. Perhaps stories tell themselves through us? Here is a concept for a teacher of stories to learn.

And again, Anna, the proud teacher, says, *Brava, brava.*

My teaching is complicated by languages. My students' English is excellent but fails sometimes, especially on technicality, and I do not have the capacity to explain myself in Italian. We end up spending much of our time fishing together for words in either language and even sometimes in French, which one of the students speaks perfectly. She translates for me when necessary but I count it a failure.

I come home on the train in the late evening counting the stations: Genova Quarto Dei Mille, Genova Quinto, Genova Nervi, Bogliasco, Sori, Recco. All the announcements: we are now approaching Genova Quinto; the train for Sestri Levante is on platform two, please stand back from the yellow line; it is absolutely forbidden to cross the tracks.

I watch the sun go down beyond Capo Mele and the lights come on out on the deep, the navigation buoys and ships and fishing boats and net-markers and the ivory gulls floating against a sapphire sky. This ancient, unforgiving sea.

By Sori I am seeing myself and my travel companions reflected in darker tones in the window against the darkness. I arrive into the station at Camogli and already it is cold and I pull my Kashmir shawl around my shoulders. I never met the man from Bangladesh again. Some other man sells shawls in Piazza de Ferrari and works the outside tables of Caffè Molinari. The busy streets. People going home. People coming to work. Students going for pizza, people in bars. Handsome young men and beautiful girls. And then the crowd outside the Hotel Moderno Verdi, waiting for the lights to change. Then the press of the railway station and the train home. By Genova Quarto there is always a seat.

One evening, just as I took a seat vacated by a man with a briefcase who had spent the entire journey on his phone telling friends about the stupendous dinner he had eaten at a conference the night before, each dish, each wine, the location, the name of the famous chef, *Ma dai! O dio, che meraviglia*, my own phone rang. It was an Italian number so I accepted the call. To my surprise the voice was masculine; it was Guido asking whether Saturday would be a good day for our trip. I said yes. He would meet me at the port, he said, by the little kiosk. I should bring a jacket because it might be cold out there on the water. That was it. The sound of his voice pleased me. It was deep without being theatrical, like Mr Crofton in 'Ivy Day in the Committee Room'. See you on Saturday? Yes, see you.

Something between two of the students, some animus that I can't quite isolate, means that there is a constant tension, *sotto-voce* bitching and occasional shouting in the class.

When they shout their Italian is like the discharge of a machine-gun, full of repeating fricatives and alveolar trills.

And then there was the day I went to work but only one student came because there was a street protest and the others were all out marching. I tried to find out what the protest was about but the remaining student was dismissive. They are always marching, she said, they march for everything, this is why Italy is such a crap country, with crap politicians and crap everything, because nobody wants to work. The word for protest is *manifestazione*.

And later, on my way home in the afternoon I would find myself caught up briefly in the tail end of the demonstration. A forest of red flags, *'Bella Ciao'* blaring from speakers, the chanting, the menacing police lining the street. What were they so angry about? I realise I have never taken an interest in causes. Capitalism was the water I swam in all my life and I took it as universal and normal. For a time I marched with the marchers, grim-faced trade unionists with a huge banner I couldn't read from behind, red neckerchiefs and flags, the music imposing a lively step. For an instant I felt as if I belonged and there had always been the side of me that wanted to burn the system down. But I felt fake too and when I saw Via Galata on my left I slipped out into the side streets towards the station.

But these days of tension are relatively rare. There are good days too and occasionally moments of wonder. Sometimes the numinous is made manifest. As when, on a lazy afternoon in late spring, the courtyard-side window full of the musky scent of pittosporum, I abandoned any pretext of teaching because I just couldn't be doing with it and because somewhere in the back of my head a little voice said, Let the words talk, no more analysis, and because those unexplained and inarticulate tensions had eaten up the air in the room, and the noise of the traffic on the street outside had invaded my head like the rhythm of a heavy ocean wave falling on stones, I simply read to them. It was Molly's monologue. The electric attention as I let my voice enter the dreamy afternoon warmth, rambling and stopping and gaining urgency as the poetry demanded and possessed too of an urgent need to hold some vital body between my legs and to feel wanted. And someone said, To hear Joyce in your Irish voice ... And the full-throated feminine laughter at the thing: *yes when I lit the lamp because he must have come 3 or 4 times with that tremendous big red brute of a thing he has I thought the vein or whatever the dickens they call it was going to burst through his nose is not so big after I took off all my things with the blinds down after my hours dressing and perfuming and combing it like iron or some kind of a thick crowbar standing all the time he must have eaten oysters I think a few dozen he was in great singing voice no I never in all my life felt anyone had one the size of that to make you feel full up*

I have to ask Anna to translate the letter. Partly this is because my heart feels too big for my chest, as though it will expand out through me like a butterfly while my stomach is bound in iron bands; my hands are shaking. It's because I think I know what it means. She tells me that the letter says that the request for the regular payment of my gas bill from my husband's old account has been refused by the bank. It asks me to contact his bank to ensure that the bill is paid and that all future bills are paid, or alternatively, to set up another payment, or to visit a tobacconist or the post office, through which bills may be paid on a cash basis.

It's the end, I say. I don't know how to get at that account. The bill is not even in my name.

She notices the name for the first time. It is an Italian name, she says.

They're closing in on his accounts.

But maybe the account simply did not have enough money, *cara?*

She takes my hand in hers.

You can walk into the tobacconist on Piazza Schiaffino, she says, and pay it there in cash. Money does not have your name on it. Just go and pay it. Do not be afraid. Bring the wine, the sun is going down.

I am still shaking. I do not trust myself to bring both the bottle and the glasses. I bring them separately. I knew this would happen, why am I shocked? And I realise that it is the same shock I felt when his solicitor called me in, as I thought to discuss the will, but instead to inform me of the fact that some of his creditors were going to court to appoint receivers. And first I blushed. Now when I think of it I can't believe that the first emotion I felt after the death of my husband was shame because he was bankrupt. Then as I grasped the reality, the shakes. And now again, like a wind blowing through me, strong enough to unsettle the ligaments and tendons, to shiver the bones like pieces of dried wood.

She sees the shaking as I put the glasses on the table and stands and takes the trembling hand. Come, she says. But she is unsteady on her feet and I wonder if the wind has blown through her too. I take her arm and she leans against me gratefully. She leads me down the corridor. She opens a door I have never seen open before. It is a bedroom, bigger than mine directly below, with a ceiling painted with flowers including pink roses, a big mahogany double bed, a desk and chair and a large awkward-looking wardrobe in oak.

She hasn't bothered to turn on the light and the room is lit by the sunset reflected along the corridor. She looks at me and I nod.

Always remember this room is empty, she says. Always.

A sudden calm; in a storm there are moments when everything combines to create silence where there was noise.

Later, in the warm night, unable to sleep for restless pointless need, I descend past the railway bridge, down the moonlit steps of the *salita*, through the *piazzetta* and the arches and down to the silent sea. Some lines from Shelley come to mind: *Yet now despair itself is mild / Even as the winds and waters are.* He wrote it in Naples, as far as I can remember.

The steps and streets are empty. It is after midnight. I stroll out onto the pier. A solitary man is fishing with two rods into the big cut in the rocks at the back of the church. The moon is behind me, hanging in the saddle of the mountain where Ruta lies in darkness. Nietzsche was working on *Zarathustra* there – the plaque is informative. Afterwards he went to Turin where he saw a horse beaten and where he broke down. The rest is silence.

I sit and watch the fisherman for a time. He glances back at me constantly, uneasily, surreptitiously. I feel myself swollen between the legs, desire a fierce ache in my belly. I should turn my back on him and lift my skirt and wait. I imagine it all as it happened in the Nausicaa episode of *Ulysses* between poor lame Gerty and Bloom. *A defect is ten times worse in a woman.* But Gerty didn't see it that way, with her legs open, *being bent so far back that he had a full view high up above her knee where no-one ever.*

The cool air on my legs; his short hissing breaths – I can hear them now as he reels the trace in; there would be some indeterminate fumbling and then he pulls my panties down and I step out of one leg and he takes me quickly, slightly painfully, with my hands spread against the church wall; hunger is great sauce. Perhaps I have an orgasm, only my second ever by vaginal stimulation, as the magazines say. I would wait for his huffing and thrusting to end in a half-sigh, half-moan, like a death rattle. He would try to put his arms around me but I would push him away. Then he'd pull out, or fall out and something would spill down my leg. Nothing is said until now: *Grazie* he would say, a polite man of about my age. And I would reply with the polite local phrase, *Ci mancherebbe*. It's what they say in shops. It cannot be translated, but it means something like *We'd miss it*. Don't mention it, as we say at home.

This is my fantasy to choose to be taken. But it makes me worse. I want to ease myself. I would do it there inside my jeans shamelessly if I thought he wouldn't look around. Instead I walk away. At the top by La Cage I turn quickly and glance back. He is tending his rod, adjusting the tension of the gut, not looking in my direction. The wind is rising and as I watch a wave slops out of the cut and almost catches him. I walk home up Salita del Priaro and across the railway bridge and the late train from Savona passes underneath, its carriages ghostly and passengerless. Destination Sestri Levante. Stand back from the yellow line.

My translation is good, she says, She is happy with my progress. It is interesting that you and I are lost among ordinary things. I do not know how to get my hair cut in English, or how to buy shoes, or how to buy a fish from the monger. But we understand when the words are hard because those words are our milieu. I shall make some corrections. Do I say haircut even if it is not cut?

We say hairdo. I would like to get my hair done. I have a new hairdo.

She pauses and looks at me, then shakes her head in disbelief.

How can something be a do?

She bends over my page and begins to read. She leans closer to the page than before as if her eyes were failing. Or the light. But the sun is a white ball in a blue firmament. There is no escaping it once I go outside. The lizards welcome it with stony insouciance. Cats sleep in the shade. It is the first day of May.

She makes small marks and sometimes changes words. The *Quaderni del carcere* is usually translated in English as *The Prison Notebooks*, she says. *Allora*, this is a very beautiful letter. It is addressed to his sister-in-law.

It's so sad, I say, that he's in prison and far away from his family. He says here, I don't know what to think because it was hidden from Delio that I am in prison. Who is Delio?

His eldest son, the one whom he met. Because he was incarcerated after Delio was born. He never met the second son, Iulik, who was born afterwards. I see here he is alarmed that Delio has found out about prison indirectly. This is 1930, it was already four years that the fascists kept him locked up. And he worries because, look it says here, It is properly strange that the grown-ups forget they were ever children and don't take account of their own experiences. And he says this in prison himself.

Who is this man? Why are you so passionate about him? What does he mean to you?

She shakes her head.

Dead heroes, she says. His name was Antonio Gramsci. I never met him of course.

I know. It says his name on the cover. And we live on Via Antonio Gramsci. But who was he?

A comrade, she says, long dead. If you wish to translate the introduction all will be revealed. But the important thing is that he was one of the founders of our party, and that Mussolini imprisoned him. He died in prison. He never saw his children again. And also that there is a Via Gramsci in almost every town in Italy.

I am conscious of echoes, the voices of children, the family making do, all the exigencies of absence. The mad gargling and barking of seagulls or the babble a baby makes, but it is in my head. Or in my soul. Where is my mother? For years I woke up with the question. I never wanted children; now if I had them everything would be worse, no escape from the bastard's debts, from his stupidity, sins of fathers visited on sons or daughters and all that. But still. The letter ends, I wish you a good feast-day, I embrace you tenderly. It is dated 15 December 1930. The feast in question is Christmas. She is in Moscow and he is in prison somewhere. *Ti abbraccio teneramente.* From this prison.

The phone call came before the letter. Friday morning and no teaching today. I was, as usual, too late to pick it up. The caller information said *Unknown* so I couldn't call back.

For years, opening unexpected letters or getting phone calls out of the blue, the thought had occurred to me that it could be her, my lost mother, trying to make contact again, and a wave of fantasies and expectations would wash over me: she had lost her memory, she had a second family and I had half-brothers and sisters, some trauma, some disaster, some pain, illness, hurt. Always those letters and calls unnerved me, though with time I had learned to cope. All survivors are like this.

But recently I had taken on a fifth student and I told myself the call could have been from her. I had begun to leave the phone turned on in case one of them phoned to say there was a strike or a protest, in which case it wouldn't be worth my while going in to work. In the meantime, the messages and calls from home had more or less stopped. Later, when I was in the shower I heard it ringing again, and again I was late. On the third call I was drinking a coffee standing by the window watching the sun on the neighbour's house pick out details of the trompe l'oeil that ran like a cake band around the upper floor just under the eaves. A pair of seagulls haggled over something dead on the roof.

I had the phone beside me. I picked it up and heard a male voice speaking perfect English and for a time I could not make sense of the words, because when I expect to be spoken to in one language and the person speaks another it takes some time for the brain to engage. Besides, the male voice seemed to have launched into small talk and compliments as if we had been speaking two minutes ago. The opening salvo was followed by something about young people that I didn't get. I ask the person to repeat everything from the beginning.

Slowly reality penetrates. It is the shit from Caffè Molinari.

He tells me, more slowly this time, that two of his students have expressed an interest in having a private tutorial on James Joyce but because of his political activity he is unable to give them time, he is being spoken about as a candidate for the next election and a lot of his time now is spent cultivating the right contacts and making appearances and speeches, I can't imagine how complex the strategy is, so in fact, he is asking me if I would like to teach a little as I discussed in the Caffè Molinari some time ago. And I say yes, of course, thank you so much, I have been doing some teaching and enjoying it.

Of course, he says, he has heard about that from a colleague and has received very good reports. He would very much like to discuss the programme to be covered and as it happens he is in Camogli tomorrow night to give a talk at the hotel on Lord Byron, who, as I must know, lived in the region for a time, though not on the mountain of Portofino as is often alleged, and so it would be very convenient to have dinner beforehand, if that was acceptable to me. I must be very lonely. In fact, he had been unable to find a place to stay because of the festival of the fish and would be returning to Genova by the late train ...

I have a sharp remembrance of the stains on the bed when I arrived.

No, I say, thank you, I'm having dinner with a friend tomorrow night. But thank you.

And I disconnect the call.

Afterwards I feel happy. It is a beautiful morning. Birdsong outside is a jungle. I go to the little *cantina* at the back and take the clothes out of the washing machine and carry them with the drying frame out onto the *terrazzo* and set them up in the sun. Here most things dry in an hour and the light bleaches them. I take pleasure in hanging her delicate lace panties, her fine linen blouses, her light linen trousers, her skirts and dresses. I feel a sense of intimacy, as if she were my daughter rather than my husband's mistress. I no longer call her the bitch or the *zoccola*. Or not so often. And very likely she too was a victim of his largesse. She must feel cheated now. And it was generous of her to hand me the keys. Very likely she thought I knew about the purchase.

Then I fill the Bialetti with coffee and water and put it on the gas and wait for the strangulated sound that means the coffee is made. It is a process I love. Under Anna's influence I have grown to prefer the coffee from the stovetop to the stuff that comes out of the coffee machine. The little aluminium pot, the water, the aluminium strainer, the black pack of Pellini, the pop of the gas and then the wait until the volcano erupts. At first I hated making coffee like that. The time it took and the noise and smell of burning irritated me.

But I think perhaps that my life has set into a slower pace. It feels more comfortable and maybe, though I do not dare to think in such terms when I'm sober, more authentic. The irony of feeling authentic in someone else's clothes, someone else's house, does not escape me. If this feels authentic, I think, what was it like before? I take two cups upstairs and walk into Anna's apartment and call out to her that I am there. She is in bed, as it happens, and I go in and sit by her and tell her the story of the phone call. She tells me that she has made enquiries about the shit from Caffè Molinari and it turns out that he is no longer a comrade, unlike the woman who sent me my four students, he is in fact one of those people who were comrades once and who now are in favour of big corporations, the kind of people who turn whatever direction the wind blows. Her voice drops almost to a whisper: It was suggested to me that he is courting Salvini and La Lega di Merda. Her eyes widen in shock. That I even know someone like that, *o dio*.

Like my late husband, I say. Blowing with the wind. He used to boast that he donated to all the parties. But what is this comrade thing? You tell me this person is a comrade. Berlinguer was a comrade. I heard you say *cara compagna* and at the time I thought it meant dear companion but now I know that it means dear comrade.

She stiffens, irritated. When did I say that? It's not a term of endearment you know, it's an important social relation, in the same way as one would say dear sir and one would be expressing a social relation too, or your highness if you acknowledge the existence of kings, which I do not. When did I say that?

Remember the telephone call you made on my behalf that resulted in me teaching four students about James Joyce?

Her face softens. Ah yes, she says, Maria is indeed a dear comrade. I brought her into the party when she was a student. She is still the same Maria. I love her dearly. You know, my dear, I sometimes dream that I can run. When I was a girl I was swift. Is that correct? There is a line of poetry, no? Fleet of foot? I was.

You were a communist?

Oh yes. We all were. I still am. That will not change until I die, which I expect to be soon, but not too soon I hope.

I hear the postman at the gate. The sound of the lid lifting on my neighbour's rusty postbox. I look out and am in time to see him put a letter in my box too. I have come to fear letters. I excuse myself and go down. I am calm. A letter almost certainly means trouble. But, surprisingly, I recognise the handwriting. It is from my sister.

How did she get my address?

I think to ask the postman to take it away again. To beg him to take it away. But the post is a one-way system.

I bring it up the steps and turn there looking, like a condemned woman, at the sun breaching a low bank of cloud that probably stretches to Africa. I dread taking the letter inside, as though it were a Trojan horse. What horror would spring from it? Finally, there on the top step in the shaft of sun, my hands trembling, I open it.

My sister tells me that she loves me and that she wants to help me.

I snort, surprising myself. Did I always doubt her love? Did the thought ever occur to me before?

She wants me to come home so she can enfold me in her loving and caring. She fears for my sanity and believes I have suffered a nervous breakdown. She understands completely and sympathises. There are times when she is close to it herself. She promises to find help for me. My friends and colleagues all know what's going on and at the moment they take the view that I am understandably shocked and traumatised but that I will come to my senses and act like a mature woman and allow the courts do their business, because at the end of the day that is certainly what will happen. There is no alternative. At least if I am present to make a case there is some hope of mitigating the result. But, she says, it's just reckless and childish to say I have no responsibility, because the truth is I was married to him, I picked him even though several people advised me not to, including my sister, and I was happy to lead the good life while his money was paying for it. Other people's money as it happened. And I had to remember that there were other people, families, old people whose money was invested in my husband's schemes and that I had a responsibility to them too. I cannot simply walk away. Essentially, I and he together were a household and my household spending exceeded my income. By a royal mile. Because this money really belongs to someone else, I am obliged for moral as well as practical reasons to pay them back. If I do not, she tells me, the banks and credit institutions will destroy me. I will never work again, never get a job, never get a bank loan, never be able to use a credit card. Finally, I need to understand that she personally is affected, not just in losing her only sister, but because Gerry had a lot of money invested and that money had just melted like a breath into the air. She closed again with her opening: please come home.

I am struck by the echo of Macbeth's description of the witches and how they melted, as breath into the wind. Why does this particular play persist in my memory more than others? He has no children. The air hath bubbles as the water hath. Out, out, brief candle! And I remember Anna telling me, what seems a very long time ago, that money is the fraternisation of impossibilities and that I can only exchange love for love and trust for trust, that money can buy everything except that. But my next thought is again: how did she get my address?

I sense the trap closing. It won't be long now.

And then I remember her sitting with me at the kitchen table, our father out at one of his committees, patiently correcting the spelling in my homework. And when I cried because I made so many mistakes, her arm around my shoulders.

I sit down and write her a letter.

Dear Sister, I'm desperately sorry that this trouble has fallen also on you. I'm sorry that Gerry got involved with my bastard of a husband. I'm sorry that there isn't enough money to cover his debts. I'm sorry that he was such a convincing liar. But you know the life I led. I had a three-bedroom house in a nice suburb, such as a college lecturer and an accountant might own together. I had a small car and he had a big one because his ego needed it. I loved my students, my teaching and my research and he was an accountant with his own practice. It was the good life, as you call it, but not the way you mean. Do you think I knew what the fool was doing? Do you think I know where he put whatever money he made, if he made any? Because you misunderstand me if you think I would have allowed it to happen. If I had known what was happening I would have driven Gerry away with a whip, I would have torn my bastard of a husband apart, but I did not know. I knew nothing. Do I deserve his debts? The law creates its own morality and it is considered immoral not to pay your husband's debts. But is it just? I have lost everything except what I never wanted and don't actually own anyway. I am trying to begin again.

I underlined _I knew nothing_. I finished with further apologies and signed it, and before I had a chance to change my mind I walked down to the post office and put it in the box.

Guido is waiting for me at the kiosk in the port. He has dressed for the occasion, somewhat ridiculously in my view, in red cotton trousers, deck shoes and an incongruous tan leather jacket. If he had worn a yachting cap it would have perfected the image.

He greets me with a hug and a perfunctory kiss on both cheeks. He has already bought the tickets and we make small talk as we wait for boarding. The day is beautiful. Yes. The sea is so calm, today we may see dolphins. That would be lovely. San Fruttuoso is beautiful. At this time of the year there will be very few tourists, but in summer it is insupportable. Many people walk there over the mountain. Those people who like walking. Do you say hiking? There is no road. But the pathways are beautiful. He quotes Byron who is falsely reputed to have written part of *Childe Harold* here. There is a pleasure in these pathless woods.

The boat is large, comfortable and feels safe. We leave the harbour and follow the coast of Monte di Portofino outwards. Guido names the places we pass as if I couldn't possibly know them. Up high is San Rocco, the little church and a scattering of houses, down low is Porto Pidocchio and beyond that Punta Chiappa. Here the Germans had a battery during the war but still the

Royal Navy shelled the port of Genoa and destroyed the harbour. The promontory is a special kind of rock, he forgets what it's called, but it stands out from the rock of the rest of the area.

He smiles ruefully. I also forget the name of the other type of rock, he says.

You make an excellent guide, Guido, I say.

Wordplay in Italian, he says smiling, what next?

Did you know that San Rocco is the patron saint of lepers, Guido?

Really? No, I didn't know that. The last Catholic in my family was my great-grandfather. Since then we've all been atheists.

I compliment myself quietly that I remember the word for great-grandfather – *bisnonno* – and remember that *bis* is also the word for second helpings and for an encore at the opera. Languages and their peculiarities. I never knew anything like this about French. It was always, for me, a language of study, of literature, of formality. I started Italian at the other end, at the personal, the private, the affectionate. Perhaps that is a fundamental difference in register between the two. I wonder if it has been noted by scholars.

Then we round the headland and the boat begins to pitch into the heavier seas caused by an easterly wind. The sweater I had brought, foolishly forgetting or ignoring his warning that it would be colder out here, is not enough, and I suggest going downstairs to the closed cabin. Instead he gallantly removes his leather jacket and puts it over my shoulders. When I thank him his smile is beautiful. I may yet enjoy this trip, I think. And until we land at the pier in the little harbour of San Fruttuoso, I bask in the masculine leather and aftershave smell of the jacket and the warmth it generates.

He is, he tells me, an editor at a publishing company based in Genoa, and also a journalist who writes for several Italian newspapers. Anna is writing her memoir and they will publish it. Not solely because of who she is but because he loves her and believes she has something important to say to the Italy of today. He speaks about her with awe. Did I know she had been a union organiser after the war? That she, a young woman, an art historian by training, had helped to unionise metalworkers in Naples. That the Party sent her to the most troublesome places. That she was a ferocious orator. That she had been beaten by fascists in Rome under the eyes of the police and the only reason they had not beaten her to death is because an officer of the Carabinieri who had half a conscience had intervened?

There is more that he would tell me another time.

Guido, why didn't Anna ever marry?

He shakes his head. Who knows. My father always said she was born to be, how do you say, *una zitella?*

An old maid? A spinster?

Yes, a spinster. It is a strange word.

But now we have rounded a little headland and a long narrow bay lies before us and this is San Fruttuoso. The boat pitches furiously as it turns, and then the opening line from a poem by Hopkins comes to me: *No worst there is none, pitched past pitch of grief.* Too late, I think. I'm over the grief.

And the pitching is over too as we motor into the shelter of the bay. I remember that our lecturer on Hopkins was a nun and we students used to annoy her by mispronouncing the line – *pissed past pitch of grief*. She lectured on Donne too, insisting that the poems to his mistress were an expression of married love. I wish I could explain my private joke. I try to formulate it and give up.

And San Fruttuoso really is beautiful. An early Christian monastery at the head of a little inlet, built into the hillside, a small beach in front and crystal clear water. We wander the beautiful empty rooms, the cloister and cistern and the long lightsome refectory, and then have lunch on the terrace of a little restaurant in front of the beach. Afterwards, sunburned and sleepy from the wine, we doze side by side on a shady side of the bay. The returning boat awakens us and we run for the pier. On the way home I thank him for bringing me here.

It has been a wonderful experience, I say. For all this time I have forgotten all my usual worries.

Since I lost my wife, he says, I have not taken the time to do anything other than work. Now that it comes to mind I realise I have spent the time since then trying to forget myself. I feel as if you have rescued me from a long sleep that was not of my choosing. It is a cliché, of course, but everything to do with pain has been said before. We are doomed to speak in platitudes.

Instinctively I lean against him. I'm sorry, I say, maybe it's better to sleep.

He makes a small dismissive gesture. The day must come, he says. It's how the world works.

He turns up anyway, the shit from Caffè Molinari. Did I give him my address? No, but I told him that I live downstairs from Anna. I am in bed in T-shirt and panties. I am reading the bitch's book. It has taken until now for me face it. The title, *What Is An Apparatus,* is not inspiring, but it is surprisingly interesting, suggesting a whole field of thought that had never entered my ken as a scholar in Irish studies. At about ten o'clock I hear my door buzzer. Again that shocked uncertainty. *Whence is that knocking?* It must be a mistake. But after a time it buzzes again, and then continuously, almost buzzing out a rhythm that I know. Furious, I pull on my jeans and sandals and go out. He is standing at the gate, holding a small case and playing something on my buzzer. It is only when I see the finger jabbing that I recognise it as the *habanera* from *Carmen.* I make the mistake of opening the gate to speak to him and he stumbles forward, accidentally getting one foot against the frame. He is drunk – I can smell it on him – though not blind drunk, just brazen. He has missed the last train to Genoa, he says, he has nowhere to go. He gives me a variant of the look with which we parted at our first encounter in Caffè Molinari. In the light of the street lamp there is something about the narrowness of his lips, the blank blue eyes and the straightness of his nose that reminds me of photographs of Joyce's American champion John Quinn whose barely suppressed anti-Sapphic bile probably helped sink the defence of *Ulysses* in the obscenity case against *The Little Review*. The publishers Anderson and Heap were lesbian partners (*the thought of women who seem to exude was well as bathe in piss,* he wrote). A small-minded prick. Of which there are many.

The last train to Genoa goes just after eleven, I say, if you go back to the station you'll be in plenty of time. It's only a ten-minute walk.

I put pressure on the gate but he keeps his foot against it.

He shakes his head.

Amore, he says. *Bellezza.*

He opens his arms wide but one has become hooked around the bars of the gate. *Fanciulla,* he says, then looks at his trapped arm in puzzlement.

Even in his obvious inebriety, I notice, he retains his upright stance and economy of movement. He is the most graceful drunk I have ever seen. I wonder what he was like twenty years ago when he believed in something other than his own importance.

I am a drunky man, he says.

A drunk man, I can't resist correcting him.

Yes, very drunky. I cannot go home.

I put a hand to his chest to encourage him back through the gate and he tries to kiss me and the tangled pair of us waltz drunkenly backwards to the first step, his arm sliding gracefully out of the gate as he moves, and he falls first, flat on his back on the steps, and I fall on top of him.

Immediately I am up, and he is stretching in pain. He tries to sit up and groans instead. I stare in horror as he rolls over onto his side and then onto his knees and remains there groaning. A light has come on upstairs. Michela comes out to her balcony and speaks to me in Italian.

I say I don't understand.

The shit replies, something forceful but containing the word for pain, and she says *Mannaggia*!

He is swearing under his breath. I pick up his case, resigned now to the fact that he's not going home. I hope he hasn't done any serious damage, hoping that under Italian law I am not in some way responsible. But he can sue if he likes, I think. I don't even own the flat.

Michela comes down. She is wearing slippers. She bends down and speaks to him. Her tone is comforting. She looks at me as she talks.

I explain to her as best I can, sotto voce, that I don't properly know him but that he decided to sleep with me even though I didn't want him to. I am sure that my words are burdened by terrible mistakes and cultural misunderstandings, and the sleep with me formulation is blunt, but I feel it necessary to explain the disturbance and to distance myself from it. And she understands in a flash. I sense quickly that she is on my side. I hear her talking to the shit who tells her his name is Gianni. And I hear the word *ospedale*, which I easily recognise. And then she is phoning a taxi on a big smartphone that she takes from the pocket of her cardigan.

It will be at least an hour, she says, because of the festival of the fish.

I had forgotten all about the festival. It explains why the faint soundtrack to our little waltz of desire and rejection is some sort of heavy-metal version of a song I hear frequently on radios as I walk around Genoa. A band is performing at the port.

So together we get him standing. He remains bent almost double, one hand on his back. He no longer looks or sounds drunk. Together we help him up the step. At the top we pause and at that very moment the sky erupts in a vast fireworks display. Michela's dog begins to bark and then whine, I can hear him through the open window. Michela says something, which I believe to be a curse directed at the explosions. The flashes illuminate the terrace and door and show us that the shit Gianni is in a bad way.

We lead him into my flat. Michela insists that he sit on a kitchen chair, not the couch he is heading towards. And so I find the two of them at my kitchen table. Of course I make tea because I am Irish. I imagine Anna Ferrara on the floor above, twisting and sighing on her bed of unrest, and wonder if I should bring her a cup too.

Gianni tells me that he is sorry for being such a *cazzone*, and the phrase takes me by surprise as if he had read my mind; though it does not mean the same thing as shit it is a good approximation. More correctly, I suppose, he is calling himself a giant prick. I am pleased with the equivalence and with my grasp of it. I assure him that I don't think he is a *cazzone*. Michela catches the word and chuckles quietly. She wags a finger at him and tells him, I suspect, that he shouldn't go calling on women when he has been drinking. His shrug is practised. It is not, I suspect, the first time that he used alcohol to steel himself against rejection. He fishes in the inside of his jacket and pulls out an envelope. He holds it for a moment so Michela and I can see it then he puts it back.

She wrote it, he says, and sent it to my office. My office! She tells me that she has spoken to a divorce lawyer. Cold, no? The kind of letter one would write to an employee who is being fired. Twenty years of marriage. Twenty-two actually. Imagine!

Then, appallingly, embarrassingly, noisily, he is crying, his hands over his face, tears leaking out between them, his cries like the frightened dog upstairs filling the apartment and the hall outside and drifting up the stairs.

Porca miseria, Michela says and shrugs sadly.

I don't really know what the expression means.

Anna Ferrara hears everything in this house. She must hear this childlike wailing. She probably thinks I have finally cracked. She will be disappointed in me.

After a time he shivers and shakes his head three times. He takes a large crimson handkerchief from the top pocket of his tweed jacket and dries his eyes. He does not look at me but says, in English: I wish to apologise.

No need for apologies, I say, feeling particularly Irish and hypocritical.

She's divorcing me, he says, what a bitch, after all I've done for her.

Michela doesn't like the word *bitch*.

She gets up and thanks me for the tea. She brings the cup to the sink and rinses it and puts it on the draining tray overhead. Then she turns, standing behind his back, and makes a face, points to him and makes a telephone signal by putting her closed hand to her ear. Then she says goodnight and leaves.

You do not think me attractive, he says miserably.

I am about to say, like the well-trained Irish woman that I am, No no, of course I do. But I stop myself in time. Instead I say, I'm sorry.

Anyway, he says, I hurted my back. It's no fun.

Hurt, I say. I hurt my back.

But it's the past tense?

It's the same in the past and the present.

Then how do I know when something is in the past tense?

I shrug. You just know. Context is important.

Of course, he says, context.

We stare at each other for a moment.

Then on a whim I stand up and take him by the hand and lead him like a child to the bedroom. I undress him to his vest and underpants – a process with which he co-operates fully, and, I suspect, delightedly – and fold back the duvet. I notice that, despite his obvious feeling that I am about to make sexual advances, he does not have an erection. Pain is a special kind of reality. His underpants are tiny and skin-tight. I hold his hands and help him to sit down. I tell him I will need to pay the taxi driver and I don't have any money so he tells me to take whatever I need from his wallet. I take twenty and show it to him. I help him to ease back on the bed and cover him over. I go to the kitchen and fill a glass of water and take the tramadol from the side drawer and give him two.

He watches as I turn out the light. I know what he is thinking and I know he's worrying that his back may ruin everything. And as I close the door behind me there is a sigh of anticipation. In the dark he can't know that I've left the room. I walk down the steps to the gate and cross the road and sit on the low wall there. A finger-clipping of moon hangs above the mountain. The fireworks have come to an end, the grand finale of *La Sagra del Pesce,* for which Camogli is famous and which is regularly covered by national television, as Anna told me.

It takes a further ten minutes for the taxi to arrive. I have worked out how to say what needs to be said and the driver is very happy to take the twenty euro and go home to bed.

Then I go back inside and climb the stairs and walk into Anna's flat. I will leave the door unlocked for you, she said, come when you want. I tap lightly on her bedroom door and look in but she is fast asleep. So I go to the back room and lie down and pull the blankets over my clothes and very shortly I too am asleep.

I sit with Anna because this afternoon she doesn't want to sleep. There are days, she says, when she fears being alone, not waking, what does Shakespeare say? That bourn which no traveller returns?

The undiscovered country, from whose bourn no traveller returns.

Brava, prof. From whose. That is important. English is such a language. It is careless about almost everything – spelling, verbs, plurals, tenses, everything. But from whose, from which, from whom. It is like a spoiled child that throws his food around but insists that his shirt must always be clean.

Who throws his food around.

Ma dai! That or who or which. It's impossible!

She makes the gesture of the joined hands in front of her chest, rocking them up and down, which indicates exasperation or surprise. *Ma dai,* people say and make the gesture. Sometimes just *Dai!* Sometimes they just join their hands and shake them, it says the same thing without a word being uttered and everyone understands it so.

How did your trip to San Fruttuoso go?

I enjoyed it, I say. I watch Anna. There is suddenly something comically sly about her.

Guido told me he enjoyed showing you around.

Good. I enjoyed it too.

He likes you.

I like him too.

Not like that.

I smile. What do you mean?

Come now, she says, we are women of the world.

Later I walk down to the town and see that a sailing ship has anchored off the pier, its masts and yards and furled sails silhouetted against the sunset. I try to imagine what it must have been like in the days of sail, the town racketing with the cracking of sails, the creaking of timbers, calls of men and women. On a hot July day the smell of dead fish and blood and tar. Jaunty men in the streets. Sweat. Rum. How many languages were spoken here? What marks have been left on the tongue? A man is selling strange metal toys to people seated outside La Cage. He is a pharmacist from Senegal. I have spoken to him before. He negotiates in English, French and Italian. I envy him his insouciance. He is *certain* that he will be understood. He told me so over a cup of coffee. He did calculus on a paper napkin, differentiation to prove he could teach. I told him that $d^y d^x$ was my nightmare, I hated maths. And he laughed his musical laugh. I teach you, he said, I make you love the numbers, lady. I can hear that laugh now as a mother buys one of his recycled gimcracks. The world moves, I think, and people move with it, we are all fleeing something and some people bring toys.

I am still translating letters with Anna. I wish she could be more patient, less disciplinarian. I think of Gramsci in prison. That lonely man. The father writing letters of love and advice. The child, the dutiful child, writing. All those relations of blood and distance and longing. What letters meant once, the interstices of everyday life filled with the shadows and sunlight of words written, affection, love, anger, loneliness. Dear Iulik, every moment of your life interests me. Write me a long letter. I hug you tight. It surprises me that I can sympathise with him. I feel myself at last capable of imagining another person's life, as if I had never been capable of that essential act of humanity before. It makes me happy.

I am seated at the only table inside La Cage. Outside the world is drowning, the rain driven by a south-westerly storm that falls on the stones of the beach with a tremendous roar. Coming down from the station was like waterboarding. Now, from inside the glass door, I watch the drops scattering like machine-gun fire towards Via Garibaldi, my clothes cooling slowly. The quiet sounds of an empty café. *A jet of coffee steam from the burnished caldron.* Joyce, of course. The muffled rumble of the dishwasher. He is mixed up now with the letters I am translating. Last night I dreamed that Molly Bloom was crying for her lost son Iulik.

Enrico is leaning on the bar reading a newspaper. I am eating focaccia filled with Parma ham, mozzarella and olive tapenade. At seven euro, it is the cheapest dinner I can find that isn't a bowl of pasta. Radio Swiss Jazz is playing over the speakers. 'Parfum de Gitane'. Anouar Brahem. Unmistakeable. A glass of Pigato, my favourite these days, four euro.

Idly, between mouthfuls, I turn over the pages of a book of photographs from the shelf behind me. *Faces of Camogli*. I recognise so many now, it's a surprise. There's the man from the Co-op restaurant and his son. One of the fishermen whose smile, sculpted from his face like a folded and fissured rock, has always attracted me. Dario from the bookshop smiling his warm smile, his bright eyes captured perfectly by the camera. The bookshop is called *Ultima Spiaggia* – the last beach. What does it mean? On page thirty-four I find Anna herself, standing beside her chariot. The picture is monochrome, but I think I can see a little Lenin badge on her lapel. Her stance is determined, brave, but also she seems about to launch herself in motion towards the camera. I have seen that move. She straightens, stretches, or what passes for a stretch on her fragile bones, and sets off with her head held high despite a pronounced curvature in her spine, her right hand swinging, her left cradling a handbag, a shopping bag, or a book. I feel a surge of love. Instinctively I touch her cheek. I am surprised that the word that comes to me is Italian, not English. *Carissima*. There is, I realise, simply no English word that expresses such warmth and affection. Dearest? Darling? Honey? *Carissima*. A caress in itself.

The clatter of the rain outside. This bubble of seeming-silence. Then, bizarrely, there is an actual photograph of Enrico standing at the bar with his hand on a copy of the same newspaper smiling at the photographer. I call him and point to it and he gives me a thumbs up.

A section entitled 'Friends of Camogli': smiling faces of people on holiday, sitting in bars, on the stony beach, on the low wall outside the *focacceria*, on the stone bench at the back of the church. In summer shirts, smiling, bronzed even in monochrome, I can almost see the salt in their hair.

Then, page 132, at one of the tables outside this very café, on the eastern side where people sit in the morning sun on fine days, the hard-edged summer shadows almost vertical, heat even in the monochrome stones, my ex-husband smiling out at me with his most reptilian smile, I can even see his tiny forked tongue, and beside him, her head half-turned away, in the act of turning towards him, her chestnut hair swinging, a slight blur, is his mistress, and on his other side, laughing loudly, head thrown back to show grey dental fillings in his upper left, such a big joke, is Gerry, my sister's husband, the cunting fucking bastard, the fucking traitorous cheating fucking cunt.

Gerry knew.

The fucking fucker. The bastard. The lying bastard.

And now my sister knows too. The letter. She knows he was here with them. Such a good joke. What story did he tell her? The bastard.

Rigid, every muscle locked in fury. If I had a knife I would stab someone.

I close the book. I pay the man. I walk out into the night of the deluge and the rain comes down on my head like the judgement of the ages.

Heart we will forget him, you and I tonight. Emily Dickinson who, on the contrary, did not forget. But I am no Emily. No pain is unending. One evening Anna takes me to a restaurant in the port. I accompany her chariot like a dutiful child. The owner greets her, kiss to right, kiss to left, hand-holding, smiling, and shows us to our table. Your favourite, he says, lifting, from a table with a view of the boats, the yellow Post-it that says simply *Sig.ra Ferrara*. No menu comes. Instead he sits and she talks food with him. He lists the things that are good tonight, fresh from the boat. Most of the names of fish mean nothing to me and the technical terms are confusing. I am astonished that something so homely, so ordinary as cooking can seem so alien. I make a mental note to enlarge my food and cooking vocabulary.

You have been eating badly, she tells me, I see it.

She points forked fingers at her eyes and then at me.

I see more than you think. We shall commence with antipasti.

The first small courses come quickly without any apparent order but, I suspect, as quickly as the kitchen can prepare them – a cuttlefish pâté on little rounds of toasted bread and a slice of lemon, some prawns and shrimp that appear to be raw, some deep-fried anchovies and some anchovies cured in lemon juice, mussels in their shells scattered with a little bread and garlic, little squid or octopus with the stripes of a hot grill on them. These are just appetisers. Sometimes he brings them, sometimes a beautiful girl with blond hair and bright eyes. Anna picks at it but insists I must eat. By the time it is all finished I am afraid to ask if anything else is coming. Anna watches it all like a queen surveying her dominion, picking at the pâté, two prawns, a mussel or two. There is wine too, a bottle of Pigato of course, dry and cold and perfect.

One eats well here, she said. Carlo is an old friend. He comes from a family of anarchists. When the old king visited Genoa they locked his grandfather up in prison as a precaution. In the old days around here it was all anarchists.

Mercifully I am not required to eat a pasta course. Instead, for the main course, Carlo brings a fish for each of us, cooked with a little sliced potato, olives and pine nuts. It is the first real fish I have eaten in a long time. It is delicious.

He sits with us afterwards. His English is not easy to understand. I know he is making the effort for me. My brain doesn't seem to be working properly this evening. When I manage a few words in Italian I realise that some of the words are French. *Il pesce è stato le meilleur que j'ai mangé per molto tempo.* Something like that. Everything about it feels wrong in two languages. I feel like an idiot but nobody laughs. And soon they slip into some more personal, perhaps more private, conversation and into an Italian which I cannot properly follow, rapid, intense, staccato. Suddenly Anna reaches out and grasps Carlo's hand, her bony translucent skin, the veins, the bones, the knuckles, folded over his big soft fist, his surprisingly clean and delicately shaped nails, and says something soft and low, and he touches his other hand to his eyes, wiping a tear perhaps, I could not be sure. His eyes are downcast as he begins his reply. Now he speaks slowly, hesitantly and I can understand many words, the language of grief is universal – eighteen years, a simple thing, going to play football with friends, and then something about a wall, a car and the devastating phrase, his heart stopped. Then he is saying that life is terrible, that death takes everything away, that death is a thief. I remember Guido's words, that everything to do with pain has been said before.

What they never tell you about old age, Anna Ferrara says pushing her plate away, is that its sleep is full of dreams of death. This is an injustice, since surely those who are about to die should dream of youth and happiness. The life of humans is little more than the subject matter of a satirical play.

She shifts her chair at an angle to the table and straightens her legs. Why do they set like cement when I sit still?

She lifts her glass and tilts it toward mine. A bell rings between us. Still, it's better than being dead, she says. Her airy, leaking laughter.

In the war, you know, I got used to death. Someone would be picked up. The job they gave me was to carry revolvers in my bag. I was a student of art and I always carried brushes and paints and things like that and they made me a bag with a false bottom. I went to a shoemaker in a certain place at a certain time and there was a password. It was like a bad novel. He gave me the bag. We exchanged perhaps ten words besides the password. I thought he was a surly man and I hated him. I was just a girl and you know how girls are. They make judgements. And one met such men in clandestine activity. The work was everything. But he was in the party and so he could be trusted. Then, three weeks later I heard he had been picked up. He was a Jew. I never knew. There is that wonderful essay by the English comrade Hobsbawm, if you know it, about why shoemakers are often radicals. He died in the Risiera di San Sabba. A *risiera* is a place where they mill rice to remove the skin. Do you call it husk? So that was where the Nazis took politicals and Anselmo was a political as well as a Jew. Anselmo was his name, which is not a Jewish name, because he was a communist and his father and mother were communists before him. Or anarchists. There were a lot of anarchists in those days there too, just like here. And syndicalists. I don't know how he died. Maybe they just removed the husk. Like in the painting by Michelangelo Buonarotti in the Sistine, the one of St Bartholomew holding his own skin on the day of universal judgement. The verb is to flay? And the past tense is flayed?

Yes, to flay and flayed.

Dunbar's 'Lament for the Makars' comes into my mind: *Timor mortis conturbat me.* Fear of death disturbs me. But better not to say it, because here Latin is still a lingua franca for people like Anna. It is hard to imagine nothingness here, as the tables empty, and the lights of the port glow softly outside. We will be the last to leave, I know. Carlo has been back with a sweet dessert wine for me and a bitter black liquid called Fernet Branca for Anna. She holds the glass like a phial of laudanum, but not for forgetfulness. She is remembering intensely, the look of concentration as she slips between English and Italian for clarity's sake, trying to tell me something about history, about politics, about herself.

But carrying those revolvers, she says, and passing through checkpoints. *O Dio*, I was always so frightened. I was not a brave one, you see. Two or three revolvers, they were English makes usually, or American, but once they handed me one of those German pistols with the straight handle, you could imagine where that came from. A Luger. You have no idea how heavy two or three revolvers are, especially with the bullets in them. And then someone would be killed and the next day or the day after I would come to collect the pistols again, and I would know that these were the ones that killed so-and-so, a German officer, or a collaborator. It would have been in the bulletin. The Germans liked issuing bulletins and proclamations, at least the Germans who were in Milan. I don't know if it's a German thing or a Nazi thing. We were always shooting spies, I'm sure some of them were mistakes because, of course, we were all paranoid. An error on our part meant torture, betrayal, death. One did not trifle with such outcomes.

Passwords and secret signs and safe houses and rendezvous and what to do if one's cell was compromised, if someone was taken up in a search, if documents or weapons fell into the hands of the enemy, if someone unexpectedly knocked on one's door at four o'clock in the morning. We only trusted party comrades. Even when the English sent someone we didn't trust him because he wasn't a communist. We didn't trust the Catholic resistance because they didn't have our discipline. We never even spoke to the liberals. Every time I was sent to meet someone the question was in my head: is it a trap?

Am I being followed? And what if I make a mistake? What if something I do betrays a comrade? What if I forget the password or the address? I was not allowed to write anything down. What if I forget the exact wording of the message and because I make a mistake my comrades are caught? One thing can be said of the war, it helps your memory. I invented ways of remembering things – rhymes, puzzles, associations.

Resistance is good for the memory?

Appunto.

That means correct or right? Or exactly?

Of course. Exactly. One night the Allies bombed the Corso Magenta and some of the bombs fell on the convent of Santa Maria. When I went out that morning I met a fellow student who was hurrying along. Did I hear they bombed the *cenacolo?* I mean *The Last Supper*, by da Vinci, you know? So we rushed down to see if the bomb had struck the painting. We were both art restaurateurs—

Art restorers?

Yes, that was what we studied at the university. We were terrified that the painting would have been destroyed, actually it was a *secco* because as you know he painted it on a dry wall, what a genius. But when we got to the convent there was a hole in the roof and the city council workers were sweeping the dust off the picture with their hard brooms! We told them to stop. It was funny. The Allied bomb didn't hit the painting but the street workers almost ruined it because they loved it so much they couldn't bear to see dust on it. Afterwards they put a cover over it and the next time it was bombed the building was almost demolished. And still da Vinci's *cenacolo* remained intact. For a painting that almost fell off the wall as soon as he painted it, it has had a lucky life. Even, you know, the monks made a hole in it for a door. Have you seen it? It's ridiculous. You go through the door right between Christ's legs!

After the war we should have finished the job. We held all the factories and the cities. The fascists were hiding in their houses like sick dogs. We had the guns. We should have put them all against a wall. Then we would have had a revolution instead of this slow death. I blame Palmiro Togliatti. He was our leader. I will never forgive him for that. I loved him but I cannot forgive him. We had it in our hands. We could feel it. Do you know what revolution feels like? It's like when you catch a sharp knife the wrong way round but you don't let go.

Then two coffees in tiny cups. Carlo is sitting at another table writing something on his phone. The waiters are clearing the last of the tables. The stars have come out.

I sleep badly, she says. All night I lie awake thinking about these things. When I sleep I dream bad dreams. This is the other irony of old age, that when one most wants to forget, one remembers everything. What pierces most is betrayal. Especially in love. When one places trust in another person and that person betrays it, one remembers every word.

And then there is her birthday dinner. She told me she would not be cooking. It was a mystery. I was not to bring wine. So I wore a light summer navy-blue cotton dress with subtle, almost self-pattern polka dots and a pair of sandals with heels higher than was normal for me. I liked her taste in dresses, but the sandals were a little tight. The mistress, no doubt, had more delicate feet. I remember what Anna said: what pierces most is betrayal. I have peasant feet but they are sturdy, and though I am not proud of them the way some women are, they are utilitarian in the extreme. I have walked the city of Genoa twenty times over *in borrowed sandals, by day beside a livid sea, unbeheld, in violet night walking beneath a reign of uncouth stars.* He was such a poet, old J.J. Never before was a novel so much also a poem and so true.

To my surprise the cook is Guido. Go sit with Anna, he tells me imperiously, she has the wine, she's on her *terrazzo*.

And Anna is in high form. She has a bottle of white in a cooler in front of her and some sort of elaborate cocktail. It's a Negroni of course, she says, but it's what we call a *Negroni sbagliato*, because instead of the gin he put prosecco. Gin is a little too strong for me before wine.

Sit by me here, she says, and we shall ask Guido to make you one too.

But at that moment Guido comes out with one for me. *Sbagliato* means mistaken. He has something like a gin and tonic himself. We all clink glasses. Anna is excited and happier than I have ever seen her. There will be a *primo* of spaghetti, apparently, followed by a fish course. And there is some talk about politics, but I am lost in contemplation of the sunset, an enormous copper coin declining into a thin wave of cloud or pollution, the colour suffusing the sea and the land, picking out the golds and ochres and yellows of the houses and the red-tiled roofs.

Then he disappears into the kitchen for ten minutes and emerges with a bowl of spaghetti full of tiny prawns.

I'm sorry, he says, I prepared everything too quickly.

Guido is nervous, Anna says mischievously, nudging me in the ribs.

He blushes and begins serving.

It is, he explains, *il classico*. The classic *spaghetti ai gamberi*, with the oil, the garlic, the parsley. One makes a little *fumetto* or stock by frying the prawn heads in a few teardrops of oil and then adding water and celery and cooking for twenty minutes. The prawns themselves are shelled and cooked in the mixture and then the pasta is turned into it and everything is ready.

Even I can see that he is talking too much.

This dinner is his birthday gift to her, all of her favourite foods. She refuses to divulge which birthday – after the age of sixty even communists become coy, she says. The word is *evasiva*, which can mean evasive, but I prefer coy. I cannot imagine Anna being evasive about anything.

The second course is tuna cooked fast on a grill pan and served only with rocket. According to the Italian tradition, we have had our carbohydrates. The second course is for protein. Then there are biscotti and a bottle of dessert wine, which sends Anna into ecstasies.

You should not have done this, Guido, she tells him.

Then to me, do you have any idea how much this wine costs? This is commodity fetishisation! However, I must say, it is extremely good.

In all this eating we mainly talk about food. But now, relaxing on the *terrazzo* in the early summer heat, talk turns to other things. Guido asks intelligent questions about the economic crash in Ireland and whether my husband was a victim of that, or something else. I tell him that as far as I can judge, my husband was a victim of his own avarice and stupidity. Then I apologise for the venom and they nod supportively.

But, I say, like the banks, it's possible that he would have gotten away with it for another ten or twenty years if it weren't for the crash. I don't know. In any case, his heart was killing him long before that. His arteries were almost completely blocked.

I do not tell them that I'm surprised he could even fuck his mistress. He could have died in her arms right here. I have already imagined the scenario more than once: a phone call to my home in Ireland or my office at the university, perhaps from the carabinieri or a coroner or the hospital to say, your husband died in his Italian house in the arms of his mistress. Or perhaps he had not even named me as next of kin. Perhaps word would come directly from her as the keys had. Or an anonymous letter: you will find your husband on a slab in San Martino Hospital in Genoa, thank you for lending him to me and I enclose the keys to the flat you never knew you owned.

But the conversation moves on, in Italian, to economics and politics, then Italy. One of the things that happens when you exist in a new language is that your brain gradually exhausts its resources. By the time they have reached Italian politics, though I recognise the names, Renzi, Beppe Grillo the comedian turned party leader, Matteo Salvini and the League and all the rest of it, I am watching a full moon rising over the mountain, laying a milky pavement on the sea. The boats are out. I can see the lights under the shadow of the headland. They make their net from Indian hemp and at the end of the season they simply cut the floats and let it decay naturally on the bottom. This is a protected area, a national park.

And so I am taken by surprise when Anna rises and says she is going to bed.

I'll leave you two to chat, she says. Tomorrow night is the opera. We shall all meet again there. Goodnight.

She touches my cheek and kisses the top of my head and hugs Guido, and then she's gone and Guido switches to English and pours us another glass of sweet Sciacchetrà. He begins to talk about Joyce. He has a friend who used to teach in Trieste and who once met one of Joyce's female pupils to whom he taught English. She still had her childhood notebooks complete with corrections in Joyce's hand – imagine how valuable they must be! Did I know that on every Bloomsday there is a reading of *Ulysses* in

Italian all around Genoa? He studied *Ulysses* in university but has since read it again and is still amazed that it is so good. Have I read *The Conscience of Zeno* by Joyce's friend Italo Svevo?

There was more but my concentration was gone. I had the feeling that his second reading of *Ulysses* might have begun after meeting me. The wine had possession of my head and my heart was drawn to recklessness. I found myself studying his eyes and then the way the lines around his eyes rearranged themselves when he smiled, and then his smile, his lips, the way he held his head a little to one side when talking, and how he pronounced the name James, with a sort of a slide on the J and the whole thing pronounced more like *zhems*.

Then we carried in the plates and stacked them in Anna's dishwasher, and washed and dried the glasses. And finally I said I had to go and he said he was staying in her spare room but he would walk me to my door. I did not object that it was a mere twenty steps of the stairs.

And so we walked down into the moonlit staircase and at my door he kissed me on both cheeks and then ran lightly back upstairs. I closed my door, and as in the movies, leaned my back against it and smiled. I am becoming, I realised, a cliché version of myself. Then I noticed that my heart was fluttering like a robin in a gale of wind. I am being ridiculous. One man in my life turned out to be one too many. But I can't help the excitement of being desired. That never goes away.

The world is governed, Anna says loudly to no one in particular, by people who do not pay their taxes but who think we should pay our debts. Look at them. She points at the plaque that names the sponsors of the Opera House like a judge sentencing a prisoner to be shot at dawn. Corporations, men of affairs, *i potenti, i padroni*, how many of them would rather see us all starve in the streets if only they had slaves? Except who would buy whatever they produce? We are not people, we are their consumers, their pets, their subjects.

Then seating herself peremptorily on a fake Louis XIV chair she says: now, here's some money, *cara*, go to the bar and get us two glasses of prosecco, I don't want champagne it's too expensive and overrated, prosecco is communist champagne, I can get a bottle for four euro in the supermarket, and what's the difference, I say.

People are looking and listening and some of them probably understand. As I stand at the bar I can still hear her voice. Her last words in English were: I always thought that old bastard Anatoly Lunacharsky was right to bend the Bolshoi Theatre to the will of the revolution – what is art for if not to better the lives of ordinary people? Then she is speaking Italian just as loudly and my blushes deepen. I can imagine her speaking to an assembled crowd, in a factory perhaps as Guido described it, telling them that they needed to think about how the bosses would fight and that the strike itself would change only the detail of how they were oppressed unless they had a bigger idea.

I accept the two glasses of prosecco, though here at the opera they cost a good deal more than four euro, and turn with mounting dread to make my way back through the chattering crowd. I am astonished to see her surrounded by young men and women who are clearly paying court, watched in amusement by two or three older heads, and standing slightly further back than the others is Guido. I blush when he catches my eye. We smile at each other. I hear Anna introduce me to the group. I catch the word for refugee. Anna is telling them that I am a *profuga* from the collapse of the economy in Ireland.

Immediately people turn to me with interest. They all love Ireland, they say. Someone mentions James Joyce, another Beckett, and someone else mentions *Dubliners*. I am not sure if they mean the book or the band. And Yeats and, for some reason, the *Mrs Brown* series. When they see my consternation they switch to English. They want to know about the crisis. They seem to know more about it than I do. They are watching several interesting parties, but they don't understand where the power lies. It seems to them that the big parties are identical. Is it like American politics where nothing changes no matter who is in power?

As the interval bell sounds I find Guido making his way towards me, smiling. He has been thinking of coming to Camogli, he says; like half of the people of the coast, he comes because the sunsets are famous. I agree that it is like a postcard because that is what everyone says, *è una cartolina*, that the *focaccia* – from Revello's or *In Scio Canto* – is the best and also the *farinata*, that Via Garibaldi makes a wonderful evening stroll, that the church is sweet or dear – *carina* a term I would not normally apply to churches – and all the time I am conscious of his body beside mine, lean and fit without feeling brute, at times touching as the passage narrows and again as I go through the doors into the auditorium. There he stops as the audience streams around us and leans close to me and whispers, may I take you out for an *aperitivo?* I like you very much.

The declaration moves me, its simplicity and directness and yet the old-fashioned almost formal register.

Of course, I say, smiling. Please do. I'd love it.

And then it is time for him to take his leave and go to his seat and I and Anna to ours and so he turns to Anna, led in on the arm of a young woman of that perfect Italian beauty, and he says, Anna my dear, I shall call to see you soon if I may, to discuss our project? We have some cover images we would like you to see. One or two I like very much. Anna smiles gracefully and says her memory is not what it was and she writes very slowly now and in any case her life was nothing remarkable, in fact quite boring by comparison with others, it is in fact boring her as she writes it; and he says nevertheless and so she says come for lunch on Sunday. He turns to me and smiles again and I smile back. In that moment I know I will take him to bed next Sunday, after lunch, a siesta of sex and maybe more and to hell with *aperitivi* and dates. I am hungry, but not for lunch. I can already imagine his body. And then the lights are dimming and I must hurry to my seat as the orchestra begins the first strains of '*Eh via buffone*' from Act Two of the *Don*. I have always loved opera as much as I loved jazz.

It is only when I am seated that I realise the discussion about lunch with Anna was entirely in Italian and I understood it as if it were English. I feel immensely pleased with myself. And then Anna leans against me and whispers, in that sonorous stage whisper of hers, that Guido is, how do you say, sweet on me, the statement followed by a soft, backhanded caress of the cheek. I look around, confident that the entire theatre has heard but in the darkness I see no knowing nods, smiles or frowns. Then enter Don Giovanni and his servant Leporello, the latter insisting that he is going to leave his master's service. Don Giovanni tells Leporello to get lost, he is a fool, stop annoying him. Leporello insists: no, no master, I will not stay. Listen friend, Don Giovanni says, but Leporello interrupts him: I want to go, I tell you! Don Giovanni, playing the wounded boss says: but what did I do to you that you want to leave me? Leporello: it was a thing of nothing, except that you almost killed me.

We are lying together, sweaty and sticky, still whispering caresses, *amore*, *carissima*, *carissimo*, endearments changing gender with the switch of a vowel; still attached in all sorts of places, trying to talk about love in various languages, when I hear her step on the stairs.

Guido's body. I take pleasure in how it gives me pleasure. Why did I not understand this before? Just this evening, dozing after the first round, I heard Guido in the bathroom washing and then returning to the bed, and I remembered my father cleaning the contacts on his spark plugs, the car doors wide open to let the air in, the smell of wet dog from the back seat. He had a special kind of spanner and he would remove them one by one and lay them out on a clean rag. He would clean them with a wire brush and then wash them in petrol. He had a special gauge for measuring the gap. The contacts always had to be close enough, but not too close. Sometimes he would tap the contacts closed with a hammer. When the plugs were inserted into the holes he had a torque wrench for tightening them to the right firmness. The memory makes me smile and in the darkness Guido hears the smile, the tightening of muscles, the moisture, a sigh – who knows how humans sense these things? He rolls up against me and his hand falls on my belly and begins its circular and determined motion. I shiver with anticipation.

Later, all the lovemaking done, and the talk making lives out of the darkness, weaving admissions, declarations, memories, hesitancies, fears into some sort of a fabric that we might wear again in the light, I hear the footsteps.

Her step is ambivalent unlike her personality, one step down to test the ground, followed by the other foot, then again one step. She is better on even ground. I listen as she clears the last step and catches her breath. Then I hear her coming towards my door and I jump out of bed without ceremony. I am pulling on my jeans before he asks me what's happening. Then the door buzzer sounds. She is wearing her dressing gown. It is almost midnight. I saw it on Guido's watch on the bedside table.

I'm so sorry my dear, she says, may I come in?

I lead her to a chair. She sits awkwardly, dragging her dressing gown over her legs. Sighing and making adjustments to her nightdress collar. Shifting uneasily on the chair, she taps her finger on the glass table top. She is still catching her breath. Even in the dull light I can see that she is pale. A faint smell of something like Pond's Cold Cream.

I received a telephone call about an hour ago.

She sweeps her hand across the table top as though brushing something away. The hand is trembling.

A dear friend.

Anna, are you all right?

It's just the shock. Life. It is a bad thing to live too long. One ends up friendless and disillusioned. One has no dreams left and no one to say stand straight and smile.

You've lost someone?

She is dying. That was what the telephone call was about. I haven't heard from her in more than thirty years. Can you believe it? She's old. Not as old as me. Fifteen years between us. Now it's bad news for her. Her daughter told me it's the end.

Again the finger rapping, the nail ticking on the glass.

I reach across and hold the hand that immediately transmits its neural staccato. She looks at me. Her eyesight is excellent. I imagine her seeing the water pooling in my eyes and for her sake I take a deep breath and blink it away.

You must go to her, I say, I'll drive of course.

She's in France. In Cluny, if you can believe it. What do you say? The ass of the world?

I laugh. In Ireland we say the arsehole of the world.

It's in the middle somewhere. *La France Profonde* and so on. Not much of a book that one. Have you read it? Your French is excellent. The daughter speaks very accented French, very provincial. She is a hostile person. I could hear her anger on the telephone.

Guido comes in, raking two hands through his hair. He somehow looks fully dressed even though he has no shoes and his shirt is unbuttoned to the third hole. His bright yellow socks are incongruous against the grey diamond tiles. I look at his feet for the first time and realise that they are unusually large and there is a hole in the sock at his big toe. I can see the nail. I blush and catch Anna's eye. She misses nothing.

Buona sera cara, he says, putting an arm around Anna's shoulder and kissing her gently on the forehead. Then he turns to me. What's happening tonight?

And I turn to Anna and I can see she is distracted, a grey circle around her eyes, the finger still rapping; there is something off-balance about her, and I think that this dying, more than others, is important to her. And I wonder why.

To go by the Fréjus tunnel or by Mont Blanc? Anna said Mont Blanc is beautiful and so it is decided. I pack the car with all her necessaries. Old ladies travel with more clothes, she says. But also a washbag with wallpaper roses on the outside and a variety of pills and unguents, perfume and nail polish, an emergency sewing kit and a manicure set inside. She directs me as I remove silk blouses (three), a silk jacket, a quilted down jacket, a long coat with a sheepskin collar, four skirts, three bras, nine pairs of knickers, two pashminas and five scarves, shoes, boots, bootees, sheepskin slippers. There is more. I have to fold them all into her ancient dark-green case with the combination locks. And I have to set a new combination because she can't remember the old one and it has to be done now while it is open in case I accidentally touch the tumblers and lock it forever. It is, she says, a very safe suitcase. When I lift it I wonder if it has a false bottom full of American or British revolvers and their bullets. The idea that I might be engaged in a clandestine flit across the border carrying weapons for some unknown insurgency pleases me. Let's bring the world down, I think, let it fall on our heads.

I carry it downstairs wishing that she had been young in a time of wheelie cases, then down the steps to the gate. I open the gate and make way for Michela who has overtaken me. She stops for a moment to ask if I am going home, but I explain that a friend of Anna's is ill and I'm going to drive her there. I also want to say that I *am* at home, that there is no other, but I think it better to remain silent on that matter, not to attract questions or enquiries. This is Anna's bag, I say, indicating the green monster. Michela smiles and wishes me a *buon viaggio*. She has her camera with her and from across the road she stops and turns and asks me if I'd mind if she took my picture. I smile and say of course not. So she tells me to step back into the gate. She fiddles with the camera and then takes four quick shots, standing, squatting, kneeling, portrait and landscape. She checks them on her digital screen and pronounces herself satisfied. Then she waves and says *buon viaggio* again and is off towards the steps. I imagine myself appearing in future volumes of *Faces of Camogli* as a mad Irishwoman with a huge green suitcase.

The Beetle's boot is in front because the engine, which is air-cooled, is in the back and the suitcase is a perfect fit (of course, dear, that's why I bought it). There's no room for anything else, so my own clothes go in a bin bag on the back seat.

On the way back to collect Anna I remember my mobile. I've had it on charge the past half hour, just in case. I haven't turned it on.

I lead Anna out on my arm and lock her door for her. Then, down the stairs and out to the gate. The perfume of jasmine is a catch in the throat. The Italian name *gelsomino* is more beautiful. And Gelsomina is the name of the young girl in Fellini's *La Strada*. Jasmine to Anthony Quinn's ferocious strongman Zampanò. There was jasmine in my father's garden but it never smelled like this. My mother planted it.

I ease Anna into the passenger seat and get her to hold the safety belt until I can get in. Her knees are bad today, she says, worse than most days. I click her belt in place for her, then my own and we're away. It is nine o'clock on a Monday morning and the sky is blue. I remember reading an article about how the ancient Greeks saw colour. Homer never said the sea or sky were blue. Nietzsche believed the Greeks could not even see green or blue, an entire culture of colour blindness he thought.

The Beetle roars into the early-morning crystal air and I hear Anna humming happily a song that I know is 'The Red Flag' in Italian. It has a jaunty military ring to it and I tap the wheel in time. Seeing my tapping she says, I will teach you the words, my dear. And so, in the hour or so between Genoa and Alessandria I learn to sing the old party march with gusto and delight. Someday, she tells me, it may be useful again.

I feel happy and bright. Last night I had the best sex of my life, even better than the early days with my ex-husband which, in retrospect, were not bad. It was not that Guido was especially skilful or energetic, but I found a deep maw of loneliness in me that I had not known existed, a secret pool like something I would come upon in a forest, dark and cool and fresh. Guido's tenderness was its exact complement. It was possible that I was falling in love. It was such a pleasant thought. At one point, as he lay on top of me, slowly moving, I recalled a certain winter's afternoon in my father's house, a pale sun striped by clouds, the bare bones of the chestnut tree swayed by a breeze, the sexual round of the hill beyond and the memory of happiness, of consolation, of safety was so intense that I gave a sharp cry and immediately my orgasm began. Only the second of my reign.

The roads north are not to be remembered. Carriageways packed with articulated lorries and aggressive drivers. The roadsides bleached white or grey. Even the grass has no colour. There is barely a tree or a bush in sight except scrub broom flaunting its yellow underwear at the heedless truckers. We must stop at almost every roadside service station so Anna can have a cup of coffee – in reality she needs to pee. She would order me to buy her *caffè normale*, sometimes passing me her handbag with instructions to take the money, and rush away on tottering legs headed for the sign that said *Toilette*. Then she would stand at the bar and pass remarks about the tourist junk they sold, or the quality of the pastries. Sometimes she chatted to the staff. Where are you from? Oh, I was in Riga once. I wait for the embarrassment, for her to say that she was at a party conference or something even worse in the good old days when Riga was in the Soviet Union. Instead she talks about the places she saw, the Opera House, the Freedom Monument, the beautiful art nouveau buildings, this restaurant is it still there, that bar? I watch how the barmen and women smile at her or nod agreement. How quickly they are charmed. To me they call her *la signora*. Carlo called her *la prof*. Someone else, I can't remember who, addressed her as *dottoressa*. Guido calls her *carissima* and even sometimes *compagna*. I realise I know so little about her, while already knowing a thousand random facts about her life. But the completeness and complexity of it is opaque to me.

I hear the difference in accent as I travel, some twist in pronunciation that comes from the dialects their parents or grandparents spoke. Italian with something close to a French 'r' and thicker sibilance. I realise I have come to think of Anna's crystal precision as normal. But there is no normal Italian, no received pronunciation.

A strange thought strikes me. Part of the pleasure of making love to Guido was that he liked me to hold his head, cup his cheeks in my palms, hold his hair. My ex-husband hated that most intimate of possessings. I had the sudden uncanny experience of having Guido's head in my hands instead of a steering wheel, as solid and rough and vital as a human skull, a brain, eyes, teeth, tongue. Yes, tongue. I shift uneasily in my seat.

As I come closer to the mountains the traffic falls away. Soon I am moving through glassy air in empty valleys, rivers white with limestone leach bubbling over stones, under bridges, rising roads, the mountains first in the distance and then gradually filling the sky around me as I push through steep-sided valleys, their edges cut like glass, snow still in the higher cuts. The vitreous sky, a Sèvres porcelain, cobalt blue with an icy glaze. The foreground is wooded, but the high peaks are bare and cracked.

At one point, gazing out the side window at the shards of the Alps, Anna says dreamily, I feel myself at a cinema, you know those old documentaries about mountains?

I think of Sunday after dinner, the big TV on the sideboard in the sitting room, the fire burning. My father reading *The Irish Press*. Jacques Cousteau was everybody's ideal Frenchman then, and he roamed the seas on our behalf, documenting the beauty and the danger alike.

Anna says, During the war I didn't know many people in the resistance except my professor Antonio Banfi, whom I adored. All the cells were kept well apart. We were very secretive, very disciplined because of the risk if one fell into the hand of the Germans, you know. And one day I and Banfi were walking towards the station, it was on his way home and we often talked business so to speak during those walks, and an acquaintance, a person whom I hardly knew, came up to me and said, introduce me to your friend, I'm a communist too. In those days you didn't say you were in the party, and he could have been a spy. The fascists shot communists all the time. But he knew I was one and he must have known who Banfi was. But Banfi was not at that time of the party. So what could I do?

What did you do?

I introduced him and it was all right. But it could have been fatal.

I indicate automatically to pull into the slip lane for a service station but she waves me on.

It's thirty kilometres to the next one?

Never mind. My bladder is behaving itself. There was another time, one of my most dangerous runs, when I was carrying weapons and papers. The train was stopped by the Germans. They had information about explosives and intended to search everyone. My carriage was full. I had my bag on my lap and in full view of the passengers I slipped it under my seat. Then we all went outside and were searched. They searched the carriages too, but not very well, I assume. People talk about German efficiency, but in my experience it is more a waste of energy on pointless activity. Of all things a German must appear to be doing something. I was last back on board but found the exact same people in the same places, my seat empty and my bag of contraband underneath waiting for me.

They supported the struggle?

It is not so much that they supported it. For the great mass of people any struggle is too much because their lives are set on the edge of a razor. To take any side is to risk a catastrophe. So they do nothing, paralysed by fear from both sides. When you win they are happy for you and celebrate with all the rest. But if the other side won, perhaps they would celebrate too. Or they would accept it grudgingly perhaps. In any case, I do not blame them and I never did. Resistance is a struggle between life and death, and they lived that struggle every day.

Was your friend in the resistance too? The one we are going to see.

No, she was too young. I met her after the war.

Anna says no more. Silence settles between us, or such silence as the labouring of the engine, the rattling of the frame and the rumbling of the road would allow. Not a silence, perhaps, in the strictest meaning of the term, but a lacuna. I have been following the Aosta valley, the names of places gradually morphing from Italian to French even though we are still inside the border and won't, in fact, cross it until we pass through the mountain, and now I am approaching Courmayeur where I had booked a bed for the night on Guido's advice. I sense Anna's pain and loss and I want to say something to help. But instead what I say is: Anna, I owe you a great debt of gratitude, because you saved me when I came here.

I look sideways at her and she is awake, watching the road in front, the white line and the steel impact fencing on the side, a distant tunnel entrance like a bullet hole in the rock face. The silence grows long. In the end I look at her again and see that she has fallen asleep. It is only later, waking her for the hotel, that I see her makeup is streaked with tears.

The pine-panelled breakfast room. Did you sleep? Yes very well, the air suits me. Me too. Everything is so clear. Coffee? The window looks out over a long twisted valley. The Alpine peaks gleam above them in early morning sun. Earlier I had recited Wordsworth to her about huge and mighty forms that did not live like living men but moved slowly through the mind by day and were a trouble to his dreams. She liked it and had me repeat the words so she could understand them better.

But now she is angry. She says, All those years of struggle, the friends who died, the work of education, the music, the films, everything. Everything is gone – the struggle, the politics, the comradeship, all gone.

She makes the gesture of puffing something from her fingers. The occasion of this tirade is a ticker tape on the television news over my head. Something I didn't catch about Matteo Renzi, the prime minister.

In any case, he's a Catholic, she says. Look at him. A refugee from the Christian Democrats.

She says the party name in Italian, *Democrazia Cristiana*, managing to give the syllables a measure of contempt close to spitting.

And soon we will have those bastards from the Lega or the Grillini who follow the clown. *Che schifo*. That is the way things go in late capitalism. Gramsci said that in bourgeois society the political struggle is reduced to a series of personal struggles between the ones who know everything and those who are fooled by their own leaders.

I say, do you know the Abbott and Costello sketch 'Who's On First'?

She shakes her head.

Well that's politics for me.

I am about to tell her you can find the sketch on YouTube until I realise that she has probably never heard of that particular website.

The coffee comes and is pronounced good and for once the pastries please her. We chat about other things for a while, the road, the mountains, people she knew who skied, how she still finds it hard to be comfortable around Germans – there are two German-speakers at the next table. But then she comes back again to the same topic: after Berlinguer, she says, there was nothing.

You loved him?

Yes.

Were you lovers?

She laughs. I told you, no, never, we were not. I don't even know if he ever had any. And I don't care. He was the finest man we ever had, such a brain and so handsome. I know to be handsome is trivial but it was part of him. You know how he died? He was giving a *discorso*, you say a speech? at a political meeting in Padua and he had a stroke. He insisted on continuing. His funeral was the biggest ever in Italian history. My heart broke that day.

And then her mood changed again. Her smile is suddenly coy and brittle. I watch the transformation with interest, wondering if this mercurial personality comes from childhood, if this was Anna Ferrara circa 1945 or something that came later. The fiery, commanding Anna I have been used to feels more comfortable.

And you don't owe me anything, she says just as unexpectedly. If anything, it is I who owe you a debt. You have given me my freedom again.

She reaches out to catch my hand.

Then the waiter arrives to offer a second cup of coffee and we both say no.

She is always stiffer in the mornings. I help her back to the bedroom and she sits by the window while I pack and lug the giant green suitcase down to the Beetle. I stop and inhale the clear sweet air. The hotel is decked with hanging baskets of multicoloured geraniums and alyssum. It hurts the eyes in the glassy morning sun.

The German couple are packing their car. They are about my age, academic-looking, like a pair I would meet at an Irish studies conference. They would be experts in Early Irish Manuscript Interpolations, or Latin and Pseudo-Latin in the Work of James Joyce. They turn as I walk past and say good morning.

In English.

Did I detect sympathy in their smiles? I try to remember which language Anna had been speaking earlier when she was reminiscing about the war and how uncomfortable she felt about Germans. But then it was quite possible they spoke Italian too. A polite nod of the head. Yeats going between his grey eighteenth-century houses. A polite meaningless word. More complicit smiles.

Anna is still sitting in the chair and doesn't appear to hear me come in even though I greet her. When I touch her she gives a little cry without moving and her hand catches mine against her shoulder. I kneel beside her.

Are you okay?

She shakes her head. No.

Do you want to go home?

No.

She begins to rise from the chair. I hold her shoulders to steady her. Then she is standing, one hand pressed to the glass of the window. Look at them, she says. She nods towards the valley below. How many thousand trees are there? And each tree is a world of its own, how many birds? And hundreds of kinds of insects and bacteria and fungi and every life form. So many millions of things, all struggling for life in that valley. And then there are the people. And only the people have evolved a society where art co-exists with murder, where the soldier makes poetry and kills, where the torturer loves opera, where the poor man shelters from the bombs and sings songs to his children. I met de Beauvoir once and we talked about absurdity. It was an interview for a newspaper I worked for. But to me it was a concept, a fascinating idea, a fashionable one even. Only now, faced with my own actual death, I see it for what it is.

Later, as I queue for the security barrier, a sign ahead warning me that the tunnel is eleven point six kilometres long and the maximum speed is seventy, when I am expecting her to pass a remark on the carabinieri hanging about with their assault rifles, whom she had previously described to me as petty fascists who would rather beat a poor anarchist to death and throw him out the window than save someone from the gas chambers, instead she says, I can't tell how many tunnels we've passed through on this road, ten, twenty, I don't know, but each time as we enter the darkness I close my eyes. I'm frightened.

I knew Dario Fo, she says with her eyes closed as I maintain a steady seventy inside the mountain, keeping two blue lights between me and the car ahead and trying not to be distracted by the tunnel markings. He was never a member of the party, but he was a comrade. He wrote that play about the anarchist they killed – Pinelli. they threw him out a window. Those were the years of lead. They were worse than the war in some ways. It was the same people trying to kill us, and again they were the state, but this time they were pious about it. They put the bomb in Piazza Fontana and they blamed us. They said we wanted to make a *coup d'état*. I went there after the bomb went off. It was a small bomb, actually. But it killed people just the same. In the war we came to an understanding about the explosive power of large bombs. But they came from the sky.

It feels as if the tunnel is narrowing, the walls leaning down on top of us. The lights exert a hypnotic effect. Has someone studied this, I wonder, the way that passing blue lights affect your perception of space and time? Ahead of me the curve seems to be shrinking, it looks as if the refrigerated truck three cars ahead will not make it through. Always three cars ahead. The neck of a womb. Going in or out? The mountain gives birth to two women, one already at the terminus of the other side. My own mother. Where did she die? I assume she is dead by now. My father is long gone. They were north and south to each other's temperament, light and dark to each other's thoughts. She walked out in a fit of elation that was the exact correlative of the darkness that possessed her at other times when she could do nothing, not even keep the house. So my father told me once in one of his very rare confidences. And who else can a child believe?

When eventually he set the Guards searching for her she was somewhere else, somewhere that could not be discovered. He always thought she went to England because he remembered seeing the boat going down the harbour that afternoon. She handed me into a neighbour just after nine, with some clean clothes, a change of nappies and the makings of several bottles and said she had a doctor's appointment and could be gone a couple of hours. Of course she never came back. The Guards were convinced that she had thrown herself into the sea, though the body never turned up.

I'm becoming morbid, I say. When there is no reply I look at her. Her head is thrown sideways against the headrest. She is fast asleep, her mouth half open. She could be dead.

And ahead, I hope for the light of France approaching at a steady seventy, the same steely blue sky, the same mountains. This tunnel is endless, I think. If we don't get out I'll know it has all been a nightmare and my ex will still be alive and hopefully not incurring unconscionable debts. And indeed there were a few hangovers along the way that I hope were bad dreams too, but probably not. And then the light comes and I am in France.

She wakes once I've passed Mâcon on the road to Cluny. The countryside interests her it seems, though it is as flat as a tea tray, fields and trees and occasional hamlets or single houses. She studies it for a time. Then she turns to me and says, I have the address in my notebook. We shall ask a gendarme. Just like the Italian ones, they always know who is dying.

You had a long sleep?

And now I have a stiff neck.

I'll get you some tramadol.

She waves her hand. Look at this place, she says. How do they vote around here? The winegrowers and the farmers? It must be a good life. And the French are not so corrupt as us Italians. Or their corruption is bigger. When things are bigger you can't see them. At least not when you're close.

Playfully, hoping to lighten things up: Anna, you talk about politics all the time, never about love.

She laughs and the laugh turns into a cough. A cotton handkerchief comes out of her handbag. When she has collected herself again she says: at my age love is as remote as the Ice Age. I have no way of recovering what it felt like. I wonder if there was love in the Ice Age?

And later she says: I was never a mother and so I have always been myself, I have always had a certain place in the world and I have never confused maternal love with truth. I can't say if it was worth the effort. Practically, it's just another way of doing the same thing. But that was the life allotted to me by the gods in whom I do not believe. I have always been afraid of waking one morning and finding myself in fragments on the floor. Do you say falling apart?

I indicate left and find myself driving through a medieval street. Somewhere in me I sense a faint trembling like a distant earthquake. *Falling apart.* I stop to ask directions, showing the name of the hotel from Anna's notebook, and I am directed right, left and left again. I drive into a big square with the ancient Cluniac monastery on my right and the Hôtel de Bourgogne directly ahead. And luckily there is a disabled parking space vacant directly in front.

In the sudden silence when the engine dies I hear Anna humming. I look at her and she seems happy. Then she sings some lines of which I can only catch the first words – *Re, re d'guera, tuc I re sun mort.* She stops and laughs. It was a song my grandfather used to sing, she says. *Re, re d'guera, tuc I re sun mort, ié mac cul d'Salussi che fa il becamort.* He was born in Asti. It's their dialect.

What does it mean?

Hmm. Kings, kings of war, all the kings are dead, except for the one of Saluzzo who plays the ... hmm. How do you say? The bird who eats the dead things?

Scavenger?

Yes. In fact it is not a nice word. I prefer ours. *Becamort* sounds more true. My grandfather used to sing it when he carried me in his arms. I have not thought of it since I was a child. I did not know that I even remembered it? I adored my grandfather. He was one of those old republicans.

His father fought with Garibaldi at Calatafimi. My *nonno* would make a little dance and sing, *Re, re d'guera, tuc I re sun mort!*

Again the laugh that becomes a coughing fit, the handkerchief, the shallow breathing. I worry about her.

At the check-in she hands over her identity card and pronounces herself glad that passports are no longer required to cross a border in Europe. Borders are for exclusion, we should abolish all of them, she says imperiously. There is a song by that great anarchist Pietro Gori that begins *La nostra patria è il mondo intero.* Translate!

I smile. This is my Anna. Our fatherland is the entire world?

Perfect, she says. And that is what I believe.

The receptionist comes back, having photocopied our documents. She smiles at the elderly lady holding court with her young companion. Do I pass for her daughter?

She needs to be helped up the stairs. She makes straight for the bathroom while I unpack her clothes. I know from the experience of Courmayeur that she likes her clothes to be unpacked even for one night. There is a connecting door to my room, which is smaller than Anna's: the children's room, or the maid's. Two single beds with iron frames, a table and lamp between them. It looks cold, forbidding, nunnish. I look out the window and the silvering evening light on the old walls of Cluny reminds me of the birch in my father's garden. A sudden memory of its yellowing white tatters of bark blowing in the breeze.

The day starts well. Hope rises before the dawn. By the time Anna comes down to breakfast I have acquired a tourist map at Reception and located her friend's house among the bric-a-brac of what was once the greatest Christian monastery in the world. Cluny, I learned from the brochure in my bedroom, was mostly to be described in superlatives; it had the finest library in Europe, had the largest basilica until St Peter's was built, was one of the richest abbeys, had the most notable theologians and was regarded as the light of the world in general. All stopped dead by the Jacobins of the Revolution, with whom I find myself in some sympathy – all this wealth was surely not what Jesus would have wanted. Jesus the Jacobin, the croppy boy, burning Cluny. I smile at the thought.

I have worked out how to get to from the hotel to the house on foot. It's not too far. I plan to walk her around the square first. There's a nice-looking café on the far side if she needs to sit down. I feel like I have a plan. And I am enjoying my first proper croissant in months. Even by comparison with Ireland, the croissants in Italy are shite. On the other hand, French coffee is hardly worthy of the name. I think of sitting in the sunshine at La Cage, watching the bright sea beating against the pier and the dark stones. Camogli really is home now. I am nostalgic for it after only thirty-six hours.

She comes down step by step. From my corner in the foyer I have a good view of the stairs, not by accident. I notice that she is wearing her best pale blue suit and a little silver brooch in the shape of two half-moons overlapping. I watch as she steps off the last tread and launches herself tentatively onto two feet, her face betraying her concentration, and makes for the table. Her small uncertain steps, the slight deviations in her trajectory, the speed with which she moves, like a blackbird on cold ground. I know her feet are sore. She sits and asks me to pour coffee from my cafetière. I know she will hate it. This woman who has filled my life for the past half year.

I think I died last night, she says. I'm sure I remember my heart stopping. It was not so bad.

By nine o'clock, when she is mobile enough to walk, the sun is already hot. I am grateful for it. I imagine it easing her bones. She insists she does not want to walk the square. It's boring, she says. It's already boring being old, but this square is even more boring.

Then what happens at the house is terrible.

The daughter lets us in and brings us to sit in a tiny dark front room among shabby oversized armchairs and a big oak sideboard lined with family photos including the obligatory grand-aunt-like stiff-collared shrew and domineering moustachioed grand-uncle, merchant class. And in one corner, out of Anna's view, but clear from where I sit, is a colour photo of a young woman in an emerald green dress. I fight back tears. Stupid, stupid, I think. I did not pay attention. I recall Anna pointing her out, the young woman walking in the sea. She left abruptly afterwards without explanation. The dress was the trigger.

The daughter excuses herself and leaves. She reminds me of someone but I am too bothered about Anna to think. The room smells of woodworm dust and soot-falls. Anna shrinks into the huge chair, her tiny frame absorbed as into a giant stomach. Her feet do not touch the ground. We wait together for the daughter to come back. Her French was too rapid, and slightly accented, and I don't think Anna, suffering from some sort of nervous exhaustion already by half past nine in the morning, caught what was being said. But I heard it clearly enough. She was going to find a letter. We were to wait. Now I can hear her moving around upstairs, the old timbers creaking, drawers opening and closing. I want to say that something feels bad about this. It does not feel like the house of a sick woman.

What is happening, Kate?

She's upstairs.

Who?

The daughter.

Whose daughter? Yours?

The door opens and the daughter comes in. She makes her way solemnly, wordlessly, to stand in front of Anna. Anna looks from her to me. She is panicked. It's clear she doesn't recognise the woman, or understand what's going on. She is shocked, disorientated, traumatised in some way. I am about to explain when the daughter speaks, in slow, careful French. I sense that the speech has been prepared.

Madame, many years ago, when I was fourteen, my mother entrusted a letter to me to bring to the post. She warned me that I was not to let my father see it or see me going to the post. I was to buy a stamp for Italy and post the letter and then come home and tell her what I had done. I saw that the letter was simply addressed to A. Ferrara. I surmised that it was a letter to a lover and I knew that Mama was very unhappy, and that she and my father did not have sexual relations because they slept in separate rooms. Besides, my bedroom was directly above hers and these old houses are like drums. I heard them argue all the time. I surmised, as one does as a fourteen-year-old girl, that my mother intended to run away with this A. Ferrara. And so I bought the stamp, because I did not know how much a stamp for Italy would cost, and I put it on the letter, but I never posted the letter. I brought it home and hid it. I did not open it.

Two years ago my mother was diagnosed with cancer. It had metastasised. It was to be a long struggle for her. But at the time she told me the diagnosis I remembered the letter. I have never married, you see, and although I moved to the bigger room after my father died, my old room was left much as it was. The clothes of my childhood days were still in there. I could not find the letter at first. I had mistaken where I put it. Memory plays such tricks. But when I did find it, it was open. It had been opened with a knife. Only my mother ever did that. Then she put it back and never said a word to me.

O Dio, Anna says.

And so when she died …

No!

I found an address book with your name and telephone number. It was at a newspaper and fortunately I encountered immediately someone who spoke French. I explained what was happening and she gave me your number. That is how I found you.

But you said she was dying.

You may have misunderstood. I said she was dead.

My Mathilde.

It is almost a whisper. I look at her and she is ashen-faced, her eyes big, her right fist closed on her knee. It doesn't close properly because her index finger will not bend fully. The knuckles are white.

Anna, how are you, are you well? I ask in Italian. But she ignores me.

You are going to give me the letter now? What if I refuse to take it?

The woman shakes her head. You will take it.

Anna stares at her. Something steely has come into her eyes.

What purpose would it serve, now that the woman I loved is dead?

Now I notice that the daughter is shaking like a leaf.

Please, she says, I owe it to my mother whom I loved. I ruined her life.

Anna struggles out of the chair. When she stands she is almost nose to nose with the daughter. For a few seconds they stand there breathing at each other, then the daughter steps aside and Anna makes for the door on her uncertain feet.

You and I are both guilty of something and that something cannot be forgiven, she says.

Madame, the daughter calls, holding the letter out. Look, your name. Please.

Anna stops and looks at the letter. There are tears in her eyes. She shakes her head and goes out the door and I am left making excuses and staring at the envelope. There are four separately folded pages in it, that light onion-skin airmail paper. The handwriting is small and neat.

I'm sorry for your trouble, I say suddenly.

Only later I realise that I spoke in English.

I am in time to see her take a wrong turn at the end of the street. I catch up with her as she stops, confused among the passers-by. She leans lightly against the timber frame of a medieval mobile-phone shop. *You and I are both guilty of something that cannot be forgiven.*

I take her arm and she grips mine firmly, that iron-fingered right hand. *Aiutami Kate, mi si spezza il cuore.* Help me Kate, my heart is breaking. Her breathing is short. I fear she may fall down there in the street. I bring her round to face the way I came, step by step, and suddenly, facing back, the sun in my eyes, I am not certain of myself. Something like the fine shell of an egg cracking and falling away. I can almost hear it in my head. For two seconds I don't know where I am. Or more accurately, who I am. This woman, holding a frail old Italian lady on her arm, walking in France. I should have a class to teach at this hour, a husband who will phone soon to say he will be late home. Anna feels hard as steel beside me, so inflexible a breath of wind would unbalance her. And without her I would fall down. People on the street would pick us up and carry us to a hospital.

Aiutami, mi si spezza il cuore. My husband died. His mistress came to my door. She gave me the keys and I ran away. My sister told me that everyone hates me. There is no going back. The keys opened the door to another way of being and the shell of this being is still glassy and inflexible. It does not properly belong to me.

My father was twenty-two years older than my mother. Did she find his old age unbearable? When he was lying on top of her at eighteen did she sigh for a young man's sex? Like in that song – 'Maids When You're Young Never Wed An Old Man'. Something so bad that she abandoned her babies. Regret and remorse are not the same thing. She did not come back because there was no coming back. Her absence was of itself irrevocable.

All the years of loss.

I embrace you. Write me long letters. Every detail of your life interests me. I kiss you, I hug you tight. From this prison.

The letter had been opened with a knife.

You and I are both guilty of something that cannot be forgiven.

My feet carry me. The body has a memory of light and shade and it has a kind of truth that words do not contain. Rue Lamartine, rue Municipale, rue Porte des Prés. They calm me slowly, at Anna's pace, a shuffling unsteady slowing of the blood. I plotted this before breakfast. There is the Hôtel de Bourgogne among its Romanesque ruins. Across the street is part of the ancient monastery, above the door, carved in the sandstone, the words *Justice de la Paix*.

I want to go home, she says.

The bells of the abbey ring the change.

The surreal certainty of motorways. In all those long hours driving she says nothing. I have the feeling that she is mastering something that happens inside. Her face betrays no emotion, but her eyes flit constantly like birds on a frosty yard. Her bloodless pallor is frightening. I dare ask nothing. I do not, I realise, have the vocabulary for loss, for love, for fate. All I can say is, I'm sorry. I say it in my head a thousand times. I press the old Beetle as hard as it will go and when I reach the hills I change down gears and turn the lights on. It is the short twilight of alpine valleys. I am driving for the border. Sometimes I look and she is asleep. In those times I sing to keep myself awake. All the old songs my father sang, working out the words by the rhyming pattern, the fighting ballads, the love songs, songs I was taught in school in Irish and English. The light passes away and the Beetle's headlamps are faint pencils in the dark of the mountain passes until I come to the tunnel entrance at Mont Blanc, and she wakes up.

Where are we?

I explain that we are on our way back to Italy, that the tunnel is just ahead. She stares at the sheer mountain, the concrete structure of the border post, the lifting barriers, the gendarmes with their assault rifles and bulletproof vests. She plucks unhappily at the seat belt and says she wants to walk. I say, no, walk on the other side, when we get through the mountain, no getting out here.

She sighs. Where are we?

I told you Anna, I say impatiently. We're returning from France. I'm taking you home. Do you know who I am?

I know who you are, she says, I'm not a fool. I liked your singing.

Then she rests the back of her hand softly against my cheek.

Amore, she says, I am in your hands. And today is your Bloomsday, no? *Ti auguro una buona festa.*

I wish you a good feast day. I embrace you tenderly. *Ti abbraccio teneramente.* The words come more easily now. I hear them in my head before I say them. Is that good or bad? How do we learn languages? Does a child hear the words in his head like an echo? Does he anticipate the masculine or feminine, modulating his articles and conforming them to the rules? Who said that language says us, not the other way round? Yes, Heidegger, the old fascist.

And it is Bloomsday. I was wrong to think I would have a class if I were still in Ireland. Time has become elastic. How long has it been since I opened the door and saw his mistress standing there? Is it true that we can shed lives the way snakes shed skin? Or are we somehow moored to the old place and time by invisible cables that draw us backwards and inwards?

I send a quick text to Guido to say where we are and that we are on the road home. Then I take the letter from my pocket and hand it to her and at that moment the truck ahead of us goes through the barrier and I roll up to pay my transit fee. A coin for the ferryman. He gives me the usual instructions, except in French this time, and hands me the same information in several languages about speed and distance and which radio station to listen to in case of emergency. From the corner of my eye I see that Anna still has the letter in her two hands on her lap, the return address facing up. Then I move forward into the black maw of the mountain and I see her raise the letter to her lips and kiss it, fold it to her chest and close her eyes. And I am hurtling through the mountain at seventy and trying not to see the lullaby of the blue lights. I am surprised that there is a slight fall towards Italy, and a very gentle curve.

Your generation, Kate, you have never experienced silence. Not the silence of impossibility.

What are you talking about?

She lifts her locket chain over her head and flicks the locket open, holding it out for me to see. Glancing left as I drive I see what looks like a twist of hair tied with thread.

What is that?

She shakes her head. As a wind in the mountains, she says, love shook my heart.

Sappho, I say softly.

She nods. You know it?

Were you two together? How did you meet?

She closes the locket and drapes the chain over her head again. She turns towards the window and stares out at the gloom of the tunnel.

Together? Such a modern word. There was no together then. Her hair was golden. So unusual here. She was an art teacher but we met at a conference. But Mathilde ... Matty was like the wind in summer. She was so happy, so strong. She had those lips, you know how the French lips are shaped in a certain way because of the *moue*, you know language shapes our faces. Hers were made to be kissed. Do you say bee-stung? I heard an Englishman say it once.

Not anymore, I say. But I was thinking, Now we say Botox.

She came to Italy so often to study. And in those days I lived some time in France. The party sent me because I spoke French. I worked with ... it doesn't matter. Matty and I, we had plans.

Sudden gulps of air. I look and see that her hand is to her throat. Tears in her eyes. I reach with my right hand and brush one away and she catches it and holds it to her cheek.

Ti voglio bene, Kate.

Anche io, I say.

The exchanges of love and affection.

Pain is an animal eating from the inside out. It needs time and distance.

Somewhere beyond midway I look again and she is asleep. I wish I'd brought a blanket for her legs because now the night is cooling fast and the ancient heater is using up the oxygen. It's more like being underwater than underground. The repeating lights bring a playground song to mind: 'One, Two, Three O'Leary'. I and my girlfriends throwing a tennis ball in the afternoon against the eastern gable of the old school. Six of us in a row.

Children playing into the shadow. Sometimes my heart breaks for the simplicity of cotton dresses and knickers, white socks and brogues. Before I knew anything. Before the world pushed its grubby finger into my head. Reality is a poison.

I come out on the other side and it is already night.

Dropping down a steep curve, a high stone wall on one side, a river on the other, she moves slightly towards me and something reptilian and primitive in the motion unsettles me too. I try to straighten the car's trajectory, but she slides again and now her head is against my shoulder, tilted at an extreme angle. I take a deep breath and exhale but it comes out as a moan.

A service area. I swing round the winding slip road and pull into the space at the farthest end where the buses and lorries go.

I take a deep breath again and check her pulse, though how pulses are found I don't know, and place my palm under her left breast for a heartbeat. I listen at her mouth for breathing. Nothing. Perhaps a faint ticking sound. I open the door and get out. The mountain air is cool, and standing under the ceiling of the universe, cursing and crying and trying to think, the thought comes to me unbidden that I loved her in a way that I may never understand. I remember the touch of her hand on my cheek and that word, *amore*.

The service station is drifting in a submarine light, a thin mist softening the edges. There is no valley, no mountain – beyond the lights there is only the night. What should I do? I can see the distant service hatch, a young man in a baseball cap. He must know what to do with someone who has died in the passenger seat of your car on the way down a mountain. But to hand her over here, like cargo from the other side. Who would bring her home?

In the end I decide to drive. At the foot of these mountains is the sea. And there will be the *carabinieri*. And a doctor will know the time of death. They will want to know why I didn't report it here. It may be an offence to drive for five hours with a dead woman in the passenger seat. Nevertheless, drive I will. There will be a bureaucratic labyrinth because in Italy there is always a labyrinth, and out of its angles and apses will emerge the horned god of death and debt, and at that moment the decision will already have been made. I will have to face my obligations, even though they are not mine but my ex-husband's. They will come for the flat and then they will have taken everything, even those things I never knew I had. I realise I no longer care. I feel strong, as though the strength that ebbed from Anna passed to me.

I walk down to the station and buy coffee from the vending machine. I need to stay awake, to think. I am glad of the technology that requires no human interaction. In the light I can see mosquitoes, tiny translucent motes drifting in my direction. Their uncertain trajectory belies their sense of purpose. I will already have been bitten many times. I'll know in a few hours. It is the pregnant females that bite. I am feeding a new generation. There is, I think, something of a Greek tragedy about the idea of descending from the mountain with a dead woman. Sophocles would have done it justice. There is no armour against grief. We either love or we do not. And if we love we risk everything. And I loved her.

But climbing back into the car I am shocked by her voice: Close the door, she says abruptly, you're letting those bastards in. They're eating me!

And she is trying to grasp a mosquito in her hand the way a child might grasp at a dust mote. The shock makes me laugh aloud. Oh God, I say, I thought you were dead!

She stares at me for a moment then bursts into high-pitched laughter. Soon I'm laughing too. And then she begins to sing: *Tra gli insetti, e le zanzare, / Bella ciao, bella ciao, bella ciao ciao ciao / Tra gli insetti e le zanzare / Duro lavoro me tocca far.* I will teach you, she says. It's a song of the rice workers who worked in the most mosquito-ridden fields, about the misery of the work. They were always women, so it is a woman's song and just right for us. Through the insects and the mosquitoes, hard is the work I am forced to do. And it ends with a look to the future: *ma verr' il giorno che tutte quante lavoreremo in libertà.* The day will come when all of us will work together in liberty. I believe that, do you? That the day must come? Listen, these are the words. Drive and I will teach you.

A text comes in and I see that it is Guido. *Ti aspetto a casa tua.* I await you at your house. I send him a heart and drive back down the slip road taking the curves easy.

Anna begins my instruction. At least the chorus is easy. I have heard it on the streets more than once. I feel as if we are marching together into the empty valley and the dark and winding road home. It is that mountain dark without moon, without stars, and we are the only car on this great drop down into Italy. The end of something but also perhaps a beginning. I believe now the day will come. This is where I live. Here, where the Alps fall down in folds and fissures to a vitreous sea. Here, where the light has the character of an improbable fact. I have come through the mountain and there is no going back. Let them come and get me. I'm ready.

Acknowledgements

This is a book about friendship, love, debt, resistance, translation and communism – all of which have fascinated me for many years. It may be read as a fable and, perhaps, a love song – to Camogli, Liguria and Italy in general.

I would like to acknowledge the influence of the late Rossana Rossanda's beautiful memoir *La Ragazza del Secolo Scorso* (translated as *The Comrade from Milan*, Verso, 2020). Although the character of Anna Ferrara is not in any way based on her, I would like to think that she owes Rossana a great debt, both in terms of ideology and of spirit, a kind of debt that cannot, unlike monetary ones, be repudiated. There are also certain incidents which derive indirectly from Rossana's account of her time in the Resistance.

The booklet that Anna sets Kate to translate is a tiny collection of letters from Antonio Gramsci to his family, especially to his wife, sister-in-law and children, edited by Marco Federici Solari. It is called *Come Va Il Tuo Cervellino*.

I'm grateful to so many of my Italian friends. The following is a necessarily incomplete list: to fellow writer Daniele Serafini who read the manuscript and made many useful observations as well as patiently explaining Italian politics to me over many years; to Dr Adele D'Arcangelo and Dr Fiorenzo Fantaccini for their long friendship and advice about language, translation and other matters; to Prof Massimo Bacigalupo for many illuminating conversations about the panorama of Italian literature; to Maria Rosa Costa for much history and advice about Camogli; to Alessandra Tommei, photographer, for the use of her beautiful collection of photographs *Facce Di Camogli*; to Dr Giovanni Gozzelino for the dialect song about the dead kings as well as long conversations about dialect and Italian history and politics; to Dr Daniel O'Connell whose insights into Joyce's work, among many other things, have been a constant joy; to Dr Clare Hutton for the use of her monograph *Serial Encounters*; to Dr John McCourt from whose work I have learned much about Joyce in Italy; to Flicka Small for her observations about Joyce and food, in particular her article 'Know me come eat with me: what food says about Leopold Bloom'; and to Stefano Tettamanti, agent and translator for his advice and his friendship. Above all I am grateful to the people of Camogli for the welcome they have extended to me.